KU-524-388

Acknowledgements

My sincere thanks to all those whose recollections form the basis of this book. Also to Andy Wiggins for conducting an interview on my behalf; to Ros Kane for allowing me to use a brief extract from an interview she did; to Ken Weller and the very many other people who helped me get in touch with those people that I did interview, and who made suggestions for further reading; and to Angus Calder and Judy Greenway for reading the book in its original, longer, manuscript form, and commenting upon it.

I would also like to thank those who have allowed me to use personal photographs, copyright of which resides with them. I would like to make it clear, however, that those portrayed in the photographs are not necessarily the same as the speaker quoted underneath.

To the memory of Arnold Feldman

Foreword

When I first saw Pete Grafton's manuscript, I was interested, later enthralled – but slightly suspicious. This boat the *Dunera*, for instance – the name didn't seem to be spelt right, and I found it hard to believe the horrible story of conditions on board, and the plundering of alien detainees by regular troops.

Since then, two accounts of the internment of aliens have appeared in print. They make it clear beyond any doubt at all that the voyage of the *Dunera* was as scandalous as Pete Grafton's interlocutor suggested. One of them shows that the military commander of the ship committed to paper his view that the Nazis who formed a minority on the voyage were fine, upstanding, well disciplined types, whereas the Austrian and German Jews who formed a majority were 'subversive' and arrogant.

I will always think that the war waged by Britain, a capitalist and imperialist country, against Nazism was worth supporting. If Nazism had been left to collapse of its own internal contradictions, the lives of millions in Europe would have been shortened, stultified, mutilated or corrupted, even as compared with those they could expect under capitalism. But victory over Nazism helped the British ruling class confuse the ruled, and even themselves. The myths of the war which Pete Grafton first encountered in those ineffable fifties movies suggested that national unity had mysteriously abolished, not class distinctions, but their nastiness. The uniformly heroic British people had 'muddled through' bravely and their triumph against odds showed that prevailing middle class values were good ones.

The myth of 1940 has been especially potent. It evolved spontaneously, I think. Churchill's speeches and Priestley's broadcasts, uttered at the time, became part of it, gave it headlines and shape, though it could not stabilise until after Hitler's invasion of Russia and the entry of the USA into the war had made a 'happy ending' virtually certain.

The revolt of a few Tory backbenchers against Neville Chamberlain brought to the premiership the man chiefly responsible for Britain's disastrous defeat in Norway – but according to the myth, Churchill was somehow hoisted to his throne by the Will of

The People Out of Step
with World War II
Pete Grafton

Pluto ⚑ Press

First published 1981 by Pluto Press Ltd,
Unit 10 Spencer Court, 7 Chalcot Road, London NW1 8LH

Copyright © Pete Grafton 1981

ISBN 0 86104 360 X

Cover designed by Marsha Austin

Photoset by Photobooks (Bristol) Ltd
28 Midland Road, St Philips, Bristol
Printed and bound in Great Britain by
The Camelot Press Limited, Southampton

the People. 'Dunkirk' was one of the worst military disasters in British history, yet, thanks partly to Priestley's rhetoric, the word came to symbolise triumph. The Luftwaffe did not have planes designed to knock the RAF out of the air, nor to bomb British cities flat. But technical matters were ignored as the 'Battle of Britain' became an epic of chivalry and the negative fact that British morale had not collapsed under bombing was transformed into the positive myth that everyone had acted heroically.

When my book, *The People's War*, appeared in 1969, I was both delighted and dismayed by the press coverage it got. Delighted, because any author likes such wide publicity. Dismayed, because so many reviewers, especially in the provincial press, *either* asserted the myth of 1940 as the truth and chided me for not being alive at the time and/or for being too left-wing to accept the truth – *or*, worse still, praised me for confirming the myth. I think only one reviewer (not a left-wing one) really spotted that the core of my work, on which I'd expended most conscious effort, was to do with industry in wartime. Bored women in war jobs, striking miners and absentees, didn't fit into the Myth. So they were ignored, just as the internees of the *Dunera* were so thoroughly forgotten that I'd missed them completely while working towards my book.

So I'd recommend Pete Grafton's book warmly. It shows us so many things that have been forgotten because they 'don't fit in'. Neither the heroics of *Angels One-Five*, nor the delightful comedy of *Dad's Army*, represent the dominant strains in British life during the war years. Boredom, frustration, fear, anger, class class and again class were at least as often to the fore.

We can't do without myths. Writing my own book, I was unconsciously forging a left-wing myth, some critics would say a 'populist' one. I think now that it is the task of historians to create myths. But we need to remake the myth of 1939–45 so that the aliens herded into rat-infested camps, the socialists who, in some confusion, supported the CP-led People's Convention, the families who trekked from blitzed cities to save their lives, the soldiers who felt trapped in an inhuman military system, cannot be forgotten. To defeat Nazism, as one poet put it, meant defending the bad against the worse.

Angus Calder

If a mythical version of the war still holds sway in school textbooks and television documentaries, every person who lived through those years knows that those parts of the myth which concern his or her own activities are false.

Angus Calder, *The People's War*

The first myth it seems to me that should be dispelled is that of a fully informed crusading people determined to fight for freedom against oppression. Some of my generation boast about their sacrifice for their children, like to tell their kids what they done during the war, to save the country from Hitlerism. I cannae help but laugh, for there certainly was little praise for the volunteer. The truth is that most people had to be forced by conscription to fight – despite the greatness of the cause, despite the propaganda against Hitler. The fact is, less than a quarter of a million men had volunteered on top of the four and a half million men who were forced under compulsory conscription. The stories of sacrifice are just not true. If they did sacrifice, the war forced them to sacrifice.

Walter Morrison, volunteer

1 I said to my father "Why are you so bitter about the Jews?"

Teesside Boy In 1939, as a kid, you were still living in an age when Britannia ruled the waves. You didn't know anything about anything else. At school they taught you England was supreme. "We rule India." "The sun never sets on bloody Empire."

London Boy I was always sure an Englishman was worth possibly two Germans, at least four French, twenty Arabs, forty Italians and an incalculable number of Indians.

Teesside Boy In school there was no question of England being wrong. All it was was "Rule Britannia, Britannia rules the waves". At the same time I lived in a semi-bloody slum.

2nd London Boy Being in a Jewish family I used to hear what Hitler was doing and saying. It was nothing new to me that Hitler was saying these things because by and large the general atmosphere at school and around was similar in England. When I was at school I was continually ribbed. Even the teachers were anti-semitic. You were made to feel rotten.

German Jewish Boy In the years between 1928 and 1933 (when I matriculated) there were a lot of fights at school, a lot of anti-semitism and anti-foreign sentiment too. This was in middle Germany, in a town called Mainz. I think we had about another three Jewish children in our class and we were always being attacked. It wasn't an easy life. In fact it wasn't an easy life from my earliest childhood. When I was four I was playing marbles at school and suddenly the children burst out into saying "Just a Jewboy, Jewboy, Jewboy".

Leeds Tailor On one occasion the fascists mounted a campaign of smashing the windows of Jewish shops. They did it using catapults and pebbles. From the other side of the road they'd smash a window and hide the catapult and walk off, like ordinary passers-by. The Jewish people started putting up shutters over the windows.

Liverpool Docker The fascists played on anti-Irish besides anti-Jewish feeling in Liverpool. They done that particularly in

2 the Scotland Road area. That's all they were on – "The dirty Irish".

London Art Student There used to be street corner meetings at the corner of our street, Sebert Road, right opposite Forest Gate station. I can remember standing listening to a Communist speaker one night and a fascist the other night, and be absolutely unmoved by either of them. It meant nothing to me. I was interested in art, and that was all.

Liverpool Girl You used to have meetings twice a week in Islington Square. I think it was the fascists, or something, and the Economic League and Leo MacCrae and all them. Once there was a little van and it had "Economic League" written on it. The feller was standing on this van preaching and there's a couple of hundred people round, and you'd get fellers that didn't agree with what the other feller was saying, so the next thing was, his van was turned upside down, and there was trouble. As a kid you thought that was fun. You'd get belted if your Mum and Dad knew you'd been.

Glasgow Girl My father criticised the Jews, particularly the Governor of the Bank of England, who was Montague Norman, a Jew. On the front of *Abundance*, the Social Credit newspaper, was a colossal spider all over Britain – that was the illustration – and the face of the spider was Montague Norman. I said to my father "Why are you so bitter about the Jews?" "I'm not bitter about the Jews in general" he said, "in fact there's one or two Jews in the Social Credit movement, but they have an insular habit that keeps them together, that refuses to communicate in any way with other nations."

2nd London Boy My old man was secretary of the Conservative Association in Stamford Hill. With other Jewish Conservatives he had gone over to Chelsea Barracks to visit Oswald Mosley[1] to ask why he was being anti-semitic. Mosley assured him that he wasn't anti-semitic, that his was a fascism like Mussolini, and the only reason he was reacting anti-semitically was because Jewish people were having a go at him. And he believed this! He began to campaign amongst Conservatives to try and stop Jews being so antagonistic.

London Boy I lived in a twenty roomed house in the Highway, Stepney. It was called *The Big House*. Living in this house was four families, plus a raving lunatic eccentric old woman who used to hawk chocolate around the streets. One family, a really fantastic family were called the ————. Their mother and father had died and the elder sister, Florrie, took over the family. Two of the brothers were regular soldiers, but one was in the Blackshirts. Although I was afraid of the Blackshirts I wasn't afraid of him, even though I had seen him in his uniform.

We had a roof where you could come out of the attic window and there was a parapet and you could watch the Blackshirts marching. They had torches and uniforms. They had drums and they had armoured cars.

London Girl I lived in Dunston Buildings, Cable Street. I saw them march a couple of times. I was a bit frightened of them. Everybody said "The Blackshirts!", but everybody rushed out to see them all the same. Then there was that day my dad said none of us was to go out on the street on the Sunday.

2nd London Boy I belonged to an organisation known as the Jewish Lads Brigade – it was like the Church Army. I was at a dance one evening when all of a sudden one of the lads came in with the news of Cable Street – that Mosley had been prevented from marching. There was terrific cheers and everybody was thrilled.

Ex-Secretary, Stepney Branch Communist Party The story of Cable Street is a story that has been mis-written, mis-recorded and historically fucked about. The real reason Mosley was unable to march through the East End of London – the real opposition wasn't so much from the Jewish population as from the indigenous Catholic population of Cable Street.

Docker's Son It was alleged at the time that the fascists didn't do any damage in Cable Street, that it was, in fact, the Jews paid dockers to tear up Cable Street. It was discussed in our family. My father denied it.

Up till Wednesday, prior to Sunday, October 4, the Communist Party was opposed to the policy of stopping the march

Ex-Secretary, Stepney Branch Communist Party This history hasn't been recorded anywhere.[2] They used to say to me, what

4 will defeat Mosley is reasoned argument – they had leaflets saying this! And I used to argue back "I've got the finest reasoned argument, but the minute I go into a meeting to put it, I'm bashed over the head."

I raised the question of self-defence. I was immediately classified in the Party as a Blanquist, an Anarchist, a Puchist. The way to fight Mosley was not on the streets, we were only playing into his hands by opposing his meetings and marches – and this was the line of a lot of the official Jewish organisations, incidentally. We were supposed to urge people to join their union! They said to me – I can show you this in actual words – that opposing the march was a pipe dream. It would take half a million people to do that. In the event, that's what happened! There were half a million people there![3]

The Party, in fact, had a demonstration arranged for the very same day, in support of the Spanish democracy, organised by the District Committee of the YCL.[4] The leaflet, which I've still got, said "All to Trafalgar Square on October 4". That leaflet had to be withdrawn. There wasn't time to write a new leaflet, so they stamped on top of it "All to Aldgate".

The majority of the Stepney Branch Committee and the whole of the membership were behind me on this issue, but there had been a running battle with half the members on other issues – trade-union work versus street work – this had been a long battle throughout the years. But since the Branch members who opposed me lived in the same area, they couldn't opt out of the reality of their situation. I mean, for instance, a hundred fascists raided Stepney Green Dwellings one night, and when it came to phoning for the police all the lines were cut. By the time the police came, hundreds of people had been beaten up. It was no good telling these people "Get into your unions" – they had the physical problem of defending themselves. For this reason most of the Branch members supported me on this issue, and opposed the Party line – the District line – on Mosley.

After October 4 the Party put itself forward as the "Victors", as having led the fight, whereas in practice they had opposed it all the way through. They'd done the same thing with the Invergordon Mutiny. At the Unity conferences that were being called afterwards, in pursuit of the United Front line – "Unity Against Fascism" – they said that this was too big an issue for the Stepney branch to handle, and that the District Committee will have to take over. From then onwards they steadily undermined me. By December I had already been suspended as Branch secretary, and by March 1937 my expulsion from the Party had been proposed.

Ex-Central Committee Member, British Communist Party The Central Committee, as it was known then, used to meet every three weeks in the Grosvenor Hotel, London. I always used to sit with Tom Mann,[5] who was a mischievous old bugger. At one particular meeting Pollitt[6] was away. The story was that Pollitt had gone to the Canary Islands. This was while Chamberlain was still Prime Minister.

Churchill had made an approach to Dutt that the Communist Party should join hands to fight fascism and a unity of anybody

Dutt[7] had put forward a resolution that the Communist Party would join with anybody to fight to end the Chamberlain government and to set up a united front against fascism. I says to Tom Mann "Look, we're not in favour of this. We're in favour of unity with the Labour Party, not with the Liberals or any other groupings." So he says "Well, get up and speak. Go on. Go on." I got up and I opposed Dutt. When it came to the vote, my vote was the only vote against the resolution.

They asked me to withdraw and I refused. Dutt then says "You'll have to stay behind and we'll have a discussion with you." And old Tom Mann says "Now you're for it, you bugger. You know what they did with Arthur Horner!" – Arthur Horner[8] got sent to Moscow for 18 months for opposing the Party line. I'm about 28 years of age at the time. I'm not a polished politician. And who've I got to discuss it with? – Bill Rust, Palme Dutt, Jimmy Shields and Johnny Campbell.[9] Four high-powered politicians.

We went into a cafe. Dutt put it quite plainly "You're not going back until we've either got unanimity or you withdraw". I fought them, I must have fought them for about two hours. It finished up I withdrew my opposition and accepted. That was

6 bad enough, me doing that, but the following EC, three weeks later, Pollitt had returned and as we assembled he said "Before we start this meeting I want to draw your attention to what I consider one of the worst examples of political opportunism that I've come across." And he made a most vicious attack on me, for withdrawing my opposition when I knew I was right, and then he attacked everybody for being so silly as to think they could have unity outside of the Labour movement. So he reversed the previous decision and I got a rollocking into the bargain!

Ex-Secretary, Stepney Branch Communist Party I fought my proposed expulsion for a year, until March '38, when I was finally expelled. Immediately after my expulsion people I had gone to school with, when they saw me in the distance they crossed the road. At the time of my expulsion a very good friend of mine was about to get married. He came to see me. "Joe, you'd better not come to the wedding because if you come the rest of the Party members can't attend." My wife was approached – (we weren't married at the time) – and was told that if she wanted to remain a Party member she'd have to leave me. This was the pressure you were under when you were a dissident. It was a racket. It was a gang.

When the war came along everything was turned on its head. Papers like the *Daily Mail* and *Express* and some other leading papers which were all behind Mosley changed their tune. Mosley was interned. The Chamberlain era had gone, Churchill was on the way in, and the attitudes to fascism changed. Anti-fascism was the thing. You were fighting a great big war against fascism.

---

[1] Fascist. Leader of the British Union of Fascists.

[2] But see *Out Of The Ghetto* by Joe Jacobs (London: J. Simon 1978). This is the speaker's own account of the period.

[3] Phil Piratin who became Communist MP for Stepney in 1945, and who disagreed with Joe Jacobs over strategy, puts the figure at 50,000. (*Our Flag Stays Red*, Thames Publications, London, 1948). No estimated numbers were given by *The Times*, nor were contained in the official police report on the incident.

[4] Young Communist League, the youth section of the Communist Party.

[5] Syndicalist. Active in the 1889 dock strike, and the industrial unrest of 1911. Jailed in 1912 for associating himself with a leaflet that the authorities considered seditious. He was later to join the Communist Party.

[6] Harry Pollitt. General Secretary from 1929–39 and 1941–56.

[7] Palme Dutt, member of the Central Committee. Party specilist in international questions.

[8] South Wales miners' leader.

[9] Bill Rust was editor of *The Daily Worker*; Campbell was industrial organiser and Jimmy Shields was a member of the Party's Control Commission.

2 It's that vivid that Sunday morning when they said war had broke out. I said to myself "What are you crying for?"

Somerset Girl I was with my mother and she was talking to someone and they must have been discussing Munich and I can remember feeling cold, a sort of fear. That's the one time I ever thought of war. It made me feel quite cold. I was 14.

Essex Boy We had things bunged through the letter box by the ARP – "What to do". I went around filling up all the cracks in the floorboards, taping up the cracks round the windows, arranging a blanket seal over the door. That was in the sitting room. That was going to be the gas room. This was 1938.

London Woman It was about 11 o'clock on a Sunday morning when Chamberlain declared war. I was indoors on my own, and the siren went at the same time. We knew it was the warning because that's what they said it would be, this up and down . . . I was petrified – rooted to the spot. It was the thought of all the things you had heard about war because my Dad used to talk about the first war.

 Liverpool Mother It's that vivid that Sunday morning when they said war had broke out. I said to myself "What are you crying for?" When I come out onto the street, everybody must have felt the same – when you looked at the people, the expression on their faces. Everything was still. There seemed to be no sound anywhere.

Course, we had some laughs. We expected once war broke out air raids and bombing. I had gone for a walk and I had our Sheila and one of the boys with me and a siren went for the very first time. I stood still. I didn't know whether to run or walk. I pushed the little pushchair over to the Mount. To go into the Mount it's up St James Road, but it comes onto a big slope – the hearses with the horses used to come down this. If you started to run you couldn't stop, so you had to trot. And when you came there, it's a big rock been hewn out – a big tunnel and then you're into the cemetery. Quite a few people made their way to this. I was thinking "Ooh, I wonder what'll happen to our Jimmy." I'd left him with Nana. This was all going through my mind and all of a sudden – you know Liverpool humour – this man says "Tomorrow's Headlines: *Making Their Own Way to the Cemetery*" Within five minutes there was a battle going on. Some people didn't think it was very funny, but there was no bombs, no planes and the all-clear went, so we went home.

3 It was like an auction affair, like a jumble sale

Liverpool Mother We had been told that if war broke out that there'd be evacuation of the children without their mothers on the Tuesday. The mothers who were going with their children, they would go on the Friday. But it was chaos. Everything was a complete flop. We left from Lime Street station. We said goodbye to the town and everybody that was in it because we never thought we'd see it for a long time.

We got the train to Chester. We were packed out. There were no facilities on the trains bringing us down – children were wetting themselves and screaming. They all had their gas masks and little bundles of clothing and their emergency rations. The emergency rations were a block of chocolate, a tin of corned beef and a tin of condensed milk. Well you can imagine children with a block of chocolate! No such thing as opening and breaking it, so it was all smeared over their faces.

We got out at Chester and we went on a short bus ride, I don't know where because of the blackout regulations. We were put in this little hall and you were just like – You know how cattle would be in a yard and you'd say I'll have that one and I'll have that? – well, if you had more than one child you didn't have a snowball's chance of getting anywhere. A friend of mine had two little girls and she was picked out by this farmer, and of course I was very glad that she'd managed to get somewhere – and this is the truth, this is no exaggeration – when she got to the place – he lived in a derelict cottage – he told her the children would sleep on the settee and she'd sleep with him. She came back that same night.

I reckon there must have been about 300 mothers and children left, with no one to take them. The officials decided we'd have to go back. There were no facilities in this little hall they'd taken us to. Let's face it, there were certain parts, certain towns that didn't want to know. It wasn't their war. It was upsetting, naturally. These big houses, they'd never had children in them and they were asked to take them. I suppose it's only human nature. We came back that same night. We got to Lime Street early the next morning and the porters opened barrels of apples for us. They were on the platform waiting to be collected for the fruit market.

After we came back they didn't try and evacuate us again. It had been such a huge flop. Mind you, there were cases where the war was used as a convenience to get rid of children and have one glorious time. It didn't matter where they went, whether they liked it or not, so long as they got rid of them. There was big money to be earned then by women.

One reason the evacuee children were disliked was because Street people felt that they'd been sent the riff-raff, and of course, in a way, they had

London Girl Some of them were very, very rough. I was privately evacuated. I was with my grandmother who came from Somerset. There was just the one school in Street and it was divided in two. The London school from Bromley-by-Bow had their own teachers and headmaster. I had to go to the London class as I was a Londoner. The two lots didn't mix. There used to be near enough war. Here in Street and Glastonbury there used to be great gangs of boys. If a couple of London boys met one of these gangs they'd have a right punch-up. There was natural dislike. There still is, to a degree. When my husband started writing his bits for the newspaper there was a bit he wrote about Londoners and it was surprising that I had one or two very snide remarks thrown at me about "blinking evacuees."

Jewish Boy Evacuated? I can tell you a story about that! I was 14 when the war broke out and I got evacuated to Norfolk. The teacher made a speech about these boys of 14, still going to school, they should go and make a war effort – right anti-semitic bastard he was – they should be working on the land, and like an idiot I sucked it all in. So I left school. I went to work on the farm. As soon as I left school I wasn't an official evacuee. So they said "Piss off." I had to find my own lodgings – at 14. Mind, I didn't work there long. I thought: this is no life – cleaning out the pigstys in the morning, then feeding the animals, and then harvesting, carrying great big bags of chaff. It was 10 bob a week. That was the going rate for 14 years of age in 1939. After three weeks I said "That's enough for me, I'm going home to mum and dad." Not that it was much of a home.

I am an unusual case of an evacuee, because I had a very, very bad experience, myself and a few others

London Boy This was an exception rather than the rule. It would be unfair to say otherwise. I was nine and a half when war broke out. I was evacuated with my sister. The journey took three or four hours. One consolation of it all, which kept our spirits up, was that amongst the emergency rations was beautiful slab chocolate. Really beautiful. Our rations were sandwiches and this chocolate. Prior to being evacuated the only country I had seen was in Essex, on the dockers' outing to Theydon Bois.

When we arrived at ————— ————— we were put into a hall. When we got in the hall most of the kids were being allocated to their places, and there was only a few of us left. We was getting a bit concerned about that. It was like an auction affair, like a jumble sale. What happened was, the local population who were going to take evacuees (and they were well paid for this, they didn't do it for patriotism or bombs), they came along and looked at you, and if they liked the look of you they took you. We were amongst the last half dozen.

We thought we wasn't going to get anyone. As they took them, they went, and you were left there in a big hall, in a strange place. Young children are not used to that. In the end a woman – I can see her now – she was a woman of about 22, a blonde, and her name was Mrs —————, and she took us. She was a very poor woman. We learned that her husband was in the army and she had a little baby. She lived in the very last house in the village – it was at least two miles from the centre of the village.

It was a very small house. There were two rooms in the front and two rooms in the back. The toilet was in the garden. A chemical one and there was a cesspool at the bottom of the garden. It was September, the weather was very good, but the cesspool was still swampy and stank. This woman was very, very good. Very good woman. The food was good. She even took the bother to walk us to school, which was a distance of two miles. The village was over-populated with children. The London kids – I don't know whether it was the delight of seeing the country – immediately declared war on the local kids and there were lots of stoning battles. I'm happy to say we outnumbered them.

But as I said, this woman not only took us to school but fetched us as well, but unfortunately, for us, I was a . . . to put it as nice as I can, a precocious child – in other words: a spoilt little bastard! I played her up so much she wrote to my mother – (and talk about fucking poetic justice, what happened afterwards) – that she could no longer tolerate me. She would keep Annie, my sister, but not me because I would throw stuff at her and tear the place up. I suppose I did it because I didn't want to be away from home at nine and a half years of age. It might be that, or that up until the age of 18, 19 when I was a guest at a military prison for a long time, I was always a bit hard to get on with. I came from a volatile district.

My contemporaries were the Butler gang and the Krays

In my school it was nothing to have a bloke come and cosh you and take your dinner money or beat the daylights out of the teacher. I'm talking about after I came home from evacuation. Anyway, this woman would no longer have us. We were then taken to another house. We were delighted because as a child it looked bigger than it was. It was a bungalow. It was fairly modern, with a big front garden, a big back garden. Part of the garden was partitioned off and they kept hundreds and hundreds of chickens. We'd never seen chickens like this . . . – Well, we'd never seen a chicken dead or alive, because chicken had never been on my fucking menu until I was grown up.

Our pleasure at seeing this place was soon crushed. The people who lived in the bungalow were called ————. There was a Mr ————, he was a local Home Guard merchant, there was a Mother ————, then they had a girl called ————, who was the local sex queen, and her younger sister, about 12, who was trying to follow in her footsteps, and they had a son called ————. Then there was me and my sister, a family called ————, who I knew from London, from my school. There was two of them. Then there was ———— and ———— ————, who were a Jewish family. Six evacuees they had. Listen how many rooms they had! They had three bedrooms and a front room. Six evacuees, three of their own and themselves. Us evacuees more or less slept in the same room.

All we ever saw of a chicken was on a Saturday when they boiled a chicken they would put various vegetables in it, they would serve the family, and then the remains of the soup would be our meal, our main meal. What made it worse, each day they would retain the pot and add water to it, but no more chicken or peas or anything else. By the second day it was just greasy water.

He was doing it for the money, the money he was getting for

"Well, we'd never seen a chicken dead or alive . . ."

us six evacuees.[1] It came to such a position that we used to wait till late at night till everybody had gone to bed and climb out the window – in fact the son showed us (the girl showed us many other things) where the food was kept for the chickens, which we were more interested in, than seeing the genital organs of a young girl! I would climb through the window and I'd get into where they kept the chicken grub, which was bread. He had greengages as well that he used to flog and I'd nick some of them and share with my sister. She was eight, by the

14 way. I wouldn't give the Jew boys none because I was anti-semitic then. I used to up them now and again.

Our families used to send us parcels of food. This was stolen as soon as it arrived

Every item was stolen. All our toys, all our clothing that would fit members of other families, and they dictated our letters. And you've got to consider, even as young as we were, we didn't want to write and tell our parents how bad it was, because in my case my old man had died, my brothers were away in the army, and my mother had enough problems without any of this. And the others, for a variety of reasons, wouldn't write to their parents. This must have gone on, all in all, for about six months.

My sister Annie had beautiful long hair and it was falling out. And my hair started falling out. And scabs were coming on our heads and bodies. It came to light some way or another and there was a big upheaval. As a result we were transferred to an evacuee hospital at a place called Waddesdon. We learned that we had malnutrition and impetigo.

We were confined to bed for a long period. Not only us, by the way, all the other evacuees in the house too. The only time we were up was for continual sulphur baths to get rid of the scabies and impetigo. And this is an interesting thing: after this happened, when I returned to ——— ———, I found that my friend ——— had been transferred to this bastard. Fortunately before ——— got in that state he came back to London with us. It was better to be bombed to death than starved to death.

---

[1] 10/6d per week for the first evacuee child, and 8/6d for every subsequent child. The average wage in 1939 varied between £2 and £3 per week.

4 I felt certain that the war was over, that we'd lost

Oxford Lad In 1940 I was working with my father on a building site, driving the lorry. My father had been in the Oxford and Bucks Light Infantry. That's how he came to be in Oxford, because he volunteered. He was from Wales. At the time of the fall of France most of the blokes on the site, including my father, reckoned we'd had it. They said the Germans had never got that far in the '14 –'18 war.

London Lad I'd just started work, and I was in work the day it came over that France fell. My heart really . . . I really felt frightened. Being Jewish I felt very nervous. The way France fell so easily – so quick.

Commercial Traveller I was travelling on the Tube to Edgware and people were getting up, making speeches. "It's about time we caved in to Hitler. When all's said and done he's doing a good job, he's murdering all these bloody Jews." They were probably fascists.

London Evacuee I saw literally hundreds and hundreds of lorry-loads of soldiers coming through the village, coming back from Dunkirk. Soldiers with no uniforms, in shirts, in a hell of a state, and they would stop in the village and people would give them tea. I felt certain that the war was over, that we'd lost. Us kids were horror-stricken, not so much at the thought of invasion or the Germans, but the fact that this was the army, the British Army. No one could defeat them in my mind. But these soldiers passing through the village were not only ragged, they were starving. The lorries were going through the village all day. Some of them were half-naked. They were in a pitiful state. You couldn't believe it was an army. The next thing there was going to be an invasion and we was going to be finished. I was sure of it.

Austrian Refugee We moved out of London because we were terrified. In those days Göring broadcast and his frequent boastful words were "We will find them, wherever they are hiding – in the East End, in Hampstead, in Golders Green" and so one was really terrified. My brother-in-law was in the Pioneers. He had to change his name because they told him "In case you are taken prisoner, you must take an English name. If you are still called ――――― they'll know you're Jewish and immediately shoot you." So he changed his name to Kirk. Most of the Germans and Austrians who were in the Pioneer Corps anglicised their names. As far as we were concerned, we weren't too worried about being interned by the British because inquiries were made from Mr Wallington, who I had known since before the war and who was our British guarantor. It turned out to be so lucky that I had this connection to England.

---

5 Churchill had the right kind of instincts "We've got to do something" and like in Germany, you immediately turn on the Jews

---

German Refugee I had been in the country 5 years when I applied for British naturalisation, in May '38. It takes 6 months before it even comes up. War broke out and all proceedings were suspended. Strictly speaking I was an enemy alien, as were my parents.

My parents were business people, who had always planned that my brother and I – there were just the two of us – should take over the business, which was three or four department stores scattered throughout Germany, the main one in Mainz. After matriculating in March, 1933, my father had arranged for me to spend a period of what is effectively an apprentice-ship at one of the major department stores in Berlin. In May I got a letter from the Personnel Chief saying that the Personnel Chief who had appointed me had been dismissed because he was a Jew. They knew I was Jewish and said they had no place

for me. They were very sorry, but no appointments could be
made.

My parents had always intended for me to spend six months in France and six months in England to learn the language, so they said to me "You might as well go to England now, things will blow over in six months time." My father arranged for me to become apprenticed as a kind of male au-pair in a down quilt factory which was situated in London.

I arrived at Dover July 30, 1933 and waddled down with my handbag to the immigration people. "No, you can't come in. Who are you? Where's your permit to stay?" "I haven't got one." "But you have to have one." I was marched straight back again, having been given permission to ring up Mr Russell, who was in charge of the factory. He negotiated with the immigration authorities to give me a 4 weeks visitor's visa. Eventually they gave me a 6 month visa – a kind of student visa, which was renewed.

After a while working in the factory didn't satisfy me, so I went to the Brixton School of Building Technology and took a four year course. After a while I realised I wasn't cut out for a builder and that I wanted to become a structural engineer. So I did strength of materials, theory of structure, concrete design and so forth and graduated in 1936 with First Class honours.

I saw the writing on the wall because of the Munich crisis, and I tried desperately to get my parents out

But England was very sticky about immigration. Jews or no Jews, persecution or no persecution, there was a very limited quota. The conditions introduced were that you had to have a British guarantor. At that time I had a girlfriend whose cousin played guarantor for my parents. They got out of Germany six weeks before the war started.

During the famous "Crystal Night"[1] my father had been arrested and interned at Buchenwald. He spent three weeks at Buchenwald until my mother got him out by bribing some Nazi authorities in Darmstadt, the local land capital. He had been pretty badly treated. He came out more dead than alive. He had to sign a piece of paper saying that he would not communicate the fact that he had been interned to anyone. Nor did they give any certificate that he had been sent to this concentration camp. The German authorities were ready to let them leave (he had signed an undertaking that he would leave) provided they handed in all their valuables. Because they weren't allowed to take anything out my mother thought "What shall I do?"

She had a couple of rings and a fur coat. I got a friend of my girlfriend to go to Germany and bring that blessed fur coat out, by wearing it. She arrived at Dover a month before my parents were due to arrive and was promptly spotted. "What's that fur coat? Doesn't look like you." She stammered "It's my fur coat." But she couldn't prove it and she spilt the beans. After they arrived my parents found themselves with a Customs court case for attempted smuggling, for they took the blame.

Our barrister very nicely explained, although he wasn't much good, that the girl had had strict instructions not to say anything because it might get back to Germany and then my parents would undoubtedly find themselves in prison. So she hadn't said anything. My parents had meanwhile arrived and their passports had been stamped "Refugees from Nazi Oppression". Would that not be sufficient? "No," said the presiding magistrate. "Confiscation of your fur coat and the two diamond rings" plus the usual customs duty which was £300 or £400 plus a £400 fine. That was all the money my parents had brought out and they paid it over and were thereafter penniless.

I had a little bit of money and we then tried to buy a house in Newcastle-upon-Tyne, where I was working. But the war broke out and the building society refused to sanction the mortgage because we were enemy aliens. We were in Newcastle-upon-Tyne when we came up before a Tribunal, like everybody else.

The Chairman was some Colonel or other. I think he was a country gent – very suspicious of Jews, but more so of people whose official affiliation was social democrat or communist

My father had always been a devout atheist and liberal social democrat. He didn't let on fortunately, on my advice, otherwise it would have made it worse. I was sent out and they interviewed my parents. My father spoke practically no English. Then I was interviewed, and then we were all interviewed again. They decided to classify me as C because I'd lived in England long enough, was familiar with British methods, the sense of fairness and justice, and my English was good. With my parents it was different.

First of all, what proof did my father have, short of my word, that he had been in Buchenwald. I appealed to the Tribunal to look at the colour of his face! Secondly, he hadn't been in the country long enough and could not be expected to have developed a sense of loyalty to Britain. Though the British were willing to stamp his passport "Refugee from Nazi Oppression" he was classified B, which meant he couldn't move outside five miles of his home. He was deeply hurt by this. I joked with him.

All my life I've had to jolly my parents up, ever since 1929 when the thing began. You've got to learn a sense of humour after a while, particularly with the British. You learn your sense of humour in Germany, first of all, but the authorities are much the same the world over. Only in England we felt that the English have developed a sense and ability of hypocrisy which is probably second to none compared with any other nation. Hypocrisy mixed with self-deception, which is a more vicious form of hypocrisy.

My parents were eventually re-classified as C. I was transferred back to London by my firm where they were designing reinforced concrete ships for the British Admiralty – a design team on which I was employed, notwithstanding me being classified as an enemy alien, I might add.

About the time of Dunkirk, a little bit earlier I believe, all enemy aliens were cleared from coastal strips, within so many miles, and this included Newcastle-upon-Tyne. My parents were given 24 hours to leave. Once again they had to leave all their possessions behind. Subsequently, a "friend" of theirs, an Englishman, who they charged with selling their goods, sold them, but for a nominal amount. There was a grand piano which he sold for ten shillings. There was a car of mine, in storage, which was also sold for ten shillings.

Then Dunkirk happened. *The Daily Telegraph* had an article

saying that Sir John Anderson[2] had sent round a circular, an order, under which all enemy aliens were to be interned – notwithstanding that all dangerous enemy aliens already had been interned. That same day I said to my firm, Mouchel and Partners "I think I'm going to be interned tomorrow." The Secretary of the firm – the big boss secretary – said to me that I deserved all I got because "wasn't it the Jews" he said "who'd put Hitler up to this – to declare war on England". I was a bit shaken by that. I joked "Look, why not the bicyclists?" – that's the old joke, you know – "They put Hitler up to it, not the Jews."

The next day on 20 June 1940 there was the famous knock on the door at 6 o'clock in the morning

A couple of detectives said "Would you please accompany us to the police station" All three of us – my father, my brother (who had come over to England six months after me in '33) and myself found ourselves under the internment books. We were all, including my mother, living in a boarding house in Finchley Road. Females were not included in that Internment Order. In London everybody was interned. They rolled over London like a swath. Each street, a few days.

We arrived at a camp which was rather overcrowded and very muddy because it had been raining like hell, even though it was June. It was a big stadium at Huyton near Liverpool. We were still with our father. A day or so later my father left for the Isle of Man where he spent the next three months playing cards. Had quite a good time and was promptly released. There was a review and all the elderly people were released. But my mother never heard from us for a long time.

It was raining like hell and we were all feeling miserable. A soldier came along to us – an ordinary soldier, and said "Look here chaps, I've heard that there are transports going and you'll be well advised to take it because you've no doubt heard that the Dutch handed over the keys of the internment camps to the Nazis." We knew this because we could buy papers in the camp. My brother and I talked it over.

We decided to join a transport to Canada, despite the fact

that the *Arandora Star*, a ship carrying internees to Canada,
had been torpedoed and sunk. It was certain in those days that
the Nazis would come over and take over the country, and it
was also quite certain, after the behaviour we had received, that
the officials would hand those keys over. Not necessarily out of
anti-semitism, but those Colonels who refused to certify my
father category C, they wouldn't have cared less, to say the
least.

The ship we set sail on was the *Dunera*. It was staffed by a
contingent of soldiers – we heard afterwards – who were being
sent out to the Far East as a punitive action. They were
crotchety soldiers who weren't much good. They had been told
we were Fifth Columnists and parachutists.

The people actually sent to the *Dunera* were a mixture from
Huyton whose passports had been stamped C, a smaller
number of Bs and some As. The As were supposed to be
Nazis. Some of them may have been fascists, and some of them
were very good social democrats or communists, whose passports were stamped A because of the Lordships – the Chairmen
of the Tribunals – who thought they were more dangerous than
any Nazis due to the Molotov pact. This was before Russia had
entered the war, and had done a deal with Germany.[3] So there
was some method in their madness.

When we arrived on the *Dunera* the soldiers were both
frightened and angry – there was Dunkirk, there was menace,
there were the Germans and here were these parachutists
arriving with their suitcases stuffed with goods, apparently. All
they'd brought with them. The soldiers were pretty cruel –
"Come on" – and kicked our behinds. All the first lot of
internees going on board had their suitcases taken from them.

**I saw, looking through one of the holds which was still open, these
suitcases being sliced open with bayonets and the contents being
thrown overboard**

Others were luckier and managed to hold onto their suitcases.
When we arrived we were downstairs in the bunk. Somebody
said to me that they were going to strip us of all our belongings.
I had a watch so I quickly took it off and put it in my pocket.

Well, those who were carrying their watches had them taken off them by the soldiers. There wasn't much you could do about it. One of the senior British captains persuaded the deck captains that he should look after all valuables. "These soldiers are quite untrustworthy. Collect all your belongings and I'll put them in a suitcase under my bunk and when we arrive at the end you can have them back." Well, we never got them back. They disappeared. The British Government subsequently paid compensation, very fairly, and I think the Captain was court-martialled.

The night before we left Britain I spoke to somebody who'd heard a rumour that maybe we were going to Sydney. I said "Maybe, maybe not, but I'm not going to pass it on." On the third day out we were torpedoed. The torpedo just missed. It grazed the hull. Then the news was passed round that the ship was going to turn round; that we were not going to Canada. The Canadians didn't want any more internees. We were going to Sydney.

My brother wept at the thought. There were a lot of hysterical outbreaks and I had to pacify half the people who were having fainting fits at our table. People were upset because Australia seemed so far away and the war didn't look like ever going to end. We thought that out there we would forever be living behind barbed wire in the desert. You have to realise that many internees on the boat were children. They were only 14 years of age, a lot of these children. It's not very nice being torn away and not knowing what you were going to. These 14 year old children weren't accompanied by brothers or fathers. I don't know how they got there, but they were there alright.

Later we sat around the latitude of Cape Town whilst constant despatches went between the British and Australian government

The Australian government refused to accept us at first, saying "You send that ship back to England, we don't want them. We know what it means – they'll want to be released." The Australians were very tough on immigration. Before the war you needed something like £1000 to emigrate to Australia, before they'd let you in. They eventually relented. "Alright, as long as they're treated as prisoners of war and it's understood they go back again, they can come." Those were the conditions.

Altogether the journey took eight weeks. The *Dunera* was not equipped to carry the numbers that it carried. It was short of food and water. As time went on it got less and less and we got undernourished – not because of anyone's malice – it was simply terrible mismanagement. We had half an hour's exercise during the day – and they had machine-gunners up there on top. That's all we had – half an hour. Otherwise we were always under deck, without daylight. At first the guards were pretty bloody-minded. When we had exercise, for instance, they used to hurry us along with their bayonets and keep us on the double.

We sent telegrams from the ship to the representatives in Britain of the British Jewry and the Home Office. There were also various people in Britain who kept on badgering away at Anderson and the others, such as Eden, about what had happened to all those internees who were at that time on the water. At first – particularly Eden[4] – they said they knew nothing.

Eden showed himself in his truest colours

Eden said nothing had happened at all. Everything was fine! All was well! He knew nothing apart from the *Arandora Star*. He was very sorry about that, he said. There had been no further shipping of internees out. He knew only too well there were! It was Peake[5] who three weeks after we left said "Yes, mistakes have been made" and that it would take months to rectify them. "You can't possibly release everybody" he said "because quite clearly there were some dangerous people amongst them." Well, as you know, not a single person was found to be a parachutist. And there we were, in Australia for the duration of the war.

---

[1] 10 November 1938. Nazi-organised burning, smashing and looting of synagogues, shops and homes, and arrest of Jews throughout Germany and Austria, following the assassination of Vom Rath, Counsellor at the German

Embassy in Paris. The assassin was a 17 year old Polish Jew, Herschel Grynsban.

[2] The Home Secretary.

[3] The Soviet Union signed a non-aggression pact with the Nazis twelve days before Britain declared war on Germany, a pact which remained in force until they were attacked in June 1941 by the Nazis.

[4] Anthony Eden, Secretary of War.

[5] Osbert Peake, Under-Secretary, Home Affairs.

---

6 The horrific time for me was when the bombs were coming down

---

Essex Farmworker The aerodrome at North Weald was a fighter station. Spitfires. My mate was dung-carting and his horse bolted. He said to me "Seen my horses?" "No" I said. That was the first day the Jerries came over. A Saturday, about three o'clock. Bombed us here. Terrible. When the German fighters were up there the Spitfires would soon get up after them: Bing! Bing! Bing! Bing! You'd have them above you. That's when I would dive in a ditch or wherever I could.

Liverpool Girl Not long after the war started a lone raider came over. We were in the street and I could hear these bangs. There was three boys from the army in the street, home on leave, and all I could hear was this Bobby Henderson shouting "Quick! Get the kids in – that's gunfire!" I'd never heard gunfire in me life, so we run in but no bombs dropped. It was 12 months afterwards before we saw anything of bombs.

London Girl I was going to get some eels, some jellied eels, up at old Jack's. In the summer he used to have an eel stall and sell ice-cream. I went up there with a basin in me hand and a new pair of stockings on. All of a sudden there was this great big crash and I run home and dived down the shelter. I tore me stockings and from that day to this I never found that basin or the two bob! This was the first bombed area, Custom House. We got the first bomb in the war, in Cundy Road.[1]

Her Mother It came on a Friday night.[2] I had a piece of fish on the electric stove. We were going down to see the kids – they were down in Somerset – and I had a load of fruit jarred up. We got bombed out. We had nowhere to go.

London Woman At one end of Odessa Road, by Forest Lane, they had built their Anderson shelters so that they backed on to one another. Very friendly – six people had done that. And a bomb hit the middle of them. Someone said "I shouldn't go and have a look if I were you." But I had to look. I couldn't help it. Ooh, it was horrible. I saw someone's brains down the side of the crater. Round Eric Road, Fowler Road, they had a bomb one day and my mum went round there and looked. She came back and said "Ooh, I wish I hadn't gone round there. They've got them all lying out on the pavement, covered over. You can see their legs." You knew you shouldn't go, but you still had to go and have a look.

2nd London Girl The horrific time for me was when the bombs were coming down. That was quite frightening, but when we went to the underground shelter that was a bit of fun and a bit of excitement. You didn't feel so isolated in a community shelter.

London Boy One reason why I developed a real hatred for the Nazis was Lord Haw Haw. His real name was William Joyce and he broadcast on the Deutschland Rundfunk. He was compulsive. You had to hear him!

3rd London Girl People used to go mad in the shelters when they listened to him. He used to say "All you people down by the Free Trade Wharf, we're going to bomb you tonight."

London Boy They used to put him on as a joke. You'd laugh at first, but a lot of things he said came true. He'd say they were going to bomb Z shed, so and so dock, and the next morning it was bombed. So you might listen to hear whether you were going to get bombed. You'd never worry if you missed Churchill on the radio, but you would worry a bit if you missed Haw Haw.

All this stuff about Churchill's speeches being morale-boosting is utter rubbish. A lot of people had no time for him. One night when I was taken to the shelter I found a bug, not that I had not known bugs before, but I really objected to an unhygienic place where there were hundreds of people, and although I was young, my feelings about Churchill were expressed through-out the shelter along the lines of "that dirty no-good bastard is sleeping in a beautiful bed tonight – why am I not?"

Glaswegian Lad Despite the resolute speeches by people like Churchill and the rest – what they were going to do to Hitler when ever they got him, and chin out, stomach in, Victory signs and all the rest, when the bombs started to fall on Glasgow, rather than people running out into the street shouting defiance at the bombers, in the area where I was in the Home Guard dozens of women with their children ran out into the street yelling and praying to God to stop it now. They were so hysterical some of our Company had to drag them from the street and shove them into the closes, or warn they'd best get into shelters.

London Boy What was uplifting was a programme which we heard every week in the shelter called *Into Battle*. It always started with the Lilliburlero. It was terrific – really stirring tune, and then they would tell you of an incident in one man's war that week – like a parachutist was shot out of his plane, his parachute was burning, he came down in a small village in France, eight Germans tried to capture him, nevertheless he killed them all, and he was spirited by the underground back to England. Another morale booster were the concerts in the shelters. Someone would get up and sing. It was really great. And then of course you'd have the propaganda, constant propaganda which were total lies.

You would have a raid where the whole district would be shattered and everybody demoralised. Then on the news they'd tell you how many enemy planes had been shot down during the raid – totally exaggerated. It has since been proved by officers of the ack-ack that some evenings they didn't shoot any down.

Then there would be the propaganda films, which showed us that we were all equal!

It would generally be a soldier who was on leave or ready for some heroic action. He would come home and go to the local village pub and meet a young woman who happened to be the squire's daughter, and the squire was a Brigadier of the '14–'18 war. The soldier would then be class-conscious, in that he was a bit frightened because of the snob value the English have. But he would find that this Brigadier is not only human, but he goes firewatching, he's in the Home Guard, he only has one egg a week – just like everyone else! All those films were like that.

3rd London Girl They were terrible. We used to go to the pictures three times a week. It would come on the screen if there was a raid on but very few people would leave their seats. The majority would stay and watch the film.

Glaswegian Lad During the blitz on Glasgow our Company was called to a densely populated working class area in Blackburn Street, where a landmine had apparently dropped. When we arrived there the entire area appeared devastated – smoke, flames everywhere and you could still hear the screams of people in the wreckage. Our first duty was to cordon off the area, to keep hysterical on-lookers (mothers, fathers and others) away. They were scrabbling in the wreckage searching for relatives. It was to save their own lives partly too. We also got the job of taking names of people reported missing.

One of the reasons for people getting hysterical was that about 300, 400 yards away there was a cinema, the *Capital* cinema, which was always open and continued its shows, even during the bombing, and had sing-songs. It's a sad reflection right enough on some of the parents, but lots of mothers and fathers obviously thought nothing would never happen in their area. They'd maybe had a bevvy and they'd stayed on in the cinema, and it was only when they heard that their area, Blackburn Street, had been bombed that then they had to come out searching for their families. We were standing with our rifles and bayonets keeping the people out, it was that bad.

I was helping carrying coffins. Sometimes two kids in a box and you could actually hear them, rattling backwards and forwards in the coffin. I was sickened with the whole situation. There was just hatred in me. I wanted to fight against people who could do this to working class men, women and children.

London Boy In Wapping a parachutist came down and apparently he was partially blinded. He'd obviously baled out of a plane. He jabbered away to the people that gathered around him in some foreign language. They assumed he was German and they smashed him to death. They learned later he was Polish, a Polish officer, which was tragic because he was like a British fighter pilot. This is common knowledge in Wapping. Many, many people will substantiate it, but of course none are prepared to say they took part in it, or saw it happen.

London Clippie I had to be an air raid warden, besides working on the buses. I had to go and dig all the people out of the bombed houses. I was at the back of Stratford when that went. I stood with a boy and we watched six of his family brought out. Six of his family he lost, in one go.

They made me go in the ARP. Don't kid yourself it was all voluntary!

London Lad Firewatching? When I was 15 I used to have to get up at 2 o'clock in the morning after working all day in the factory and walk through the blitzes to go and bloody firewatch in the factory. That was very annoying that was. Didn't like it, but we had to do it.

London Boy I joined the Auxiliary Fire Service. They had boys. You worked two nights a week. You were messenger boys. One of the great attractions was you got to wear a steel helmet, and you had a bike. I didn't have a very heroic career though, because I deserted my bike in the middle of an air raid and took shelter. Fuck the Fire Brigade.

Glaswegian Lad When I was in the Home Guard, a machine-gun company, we had a big hall where we kept the machine-guns, and obviously we had to mount a guard on it. It was myself and another two young chaps, we done the guard nearly every night in the week. We couldnae get volunteers! It was also the same in the area that I worked at the time, with firewatching. They couldnae even get firewatchers. I used to do that too at times, finding that we were the only people bothering turning up. When I joined the Home Guard I was excused quite a bit of that.

Liverpool Girl When the May Blitz[3] was at its height there was 500 planes over Liverpool, and we had no airforce. Do you know what we had to try and combat the planes? They had anti-aircraft guns going around on vans. You were more frightened of them than anything else.

London Electrician I was working and living in Liverpool at the time. By the third night they ran out of anti-aircraft shells, they were so poorly equipped. They had to send a destroyer into the beginning of the docks because Jerry was trying to blitz the docks. The destroyer fired a line along the docks to keep Jerry off the doings. Jerry had collected a hell of a lot of our landmines which had been abandoned at Dunkirk, and he developed a technique which was absolutely bloody awful if you were in it. These flaming planes came in with one of our landmines under either wing and they systematically bull-dozed by aeroplane. Although the destroyer tried to protect the docks they bulldozed Bootle, which was the living area for the dock workers. They came in with no opposition.

It was so bad in Bootle that bridges across canals, and water, electric, gas, drains, the whole bloody lot was schmozzled. You couldn't get through any of it. The people either had to get out of there or . . . I met one poor bugger I knew at the time, who'd been blitzed. He'd been bombed out and I met him three months later. He'd been living amongst the rubble, never going to work. I've never seen a man look in such a state. His face looked like a rat. He was really a nervous animal and his eyes appeared to be trying to look behind him all the time. The bomb had smashed his house and he'd lost his wife and kids – he'd just gone beyond, with the shock of such a bashing.

Bootle Docker I was bombed out on the Saturday night. I had been working all day Saturday and I didn't finish until 6 o'clock on Saturday night. I was with mother at the time (my wife and kids were in Wales) – went upstairs and got me head down.

I had an alsatian dog at the time, which never came upstairs. I felt

this weight on me legs. I woke up and saw the dog. "What's up Stalin?"

And then I could hear mother groaning downstairs. I came down and said "What's to do?" "My God," she says "It's terrible." "What?" "The air raid!" I've only got one good ear and if I sleep on that I can't hear a thing. I said "I'll go and have a look round."

We had a door dividing the living room from the back kitchen and when I went to open it the bloody thing wouldn't open. It had jammed. I forced it open, went out into the yard and had a look around. I looked to see if the warehouses at top were on fire, because I'd said to mother "If you see those on fire, get out of the road, move – that's the target area. Once they get a fire started, all around gets blasted." I looked up, but there was nothing happening there. I went in and sat down in an armchair. Mother says "I'll make a cup of tea." I says "Don't worry. Sit down, I'll make it." I goes out into the back kitchen. Gets the kettle for water. But no water. I thought "Bloody hell." And then the light went out.

We're in the dark – well, not quite dark – it's like a summer's night. I goes in the parlour and puts a shilling in the meter. Come back to try the lights, but they're not working. So gas has gone, water has gone. We'll have to do without tea. She'd put a nice white tablecloth on the table and cups and saucers. The next thing there was a bloody fearful rattle. I stuffed her underneath the couch, and then the bloody windows came in, and tons and tons of soot were falling down the chimney, and splathered all over the place and all over me. I sat in the chair with me good ear up and me bad ear down. And then I heard them: "Here we are, here we are" – that was the drone, just like "Here we are."

The beam above me fell down, right across me and I got cut. I'm underneath this beam and I hear a voice in the very far distance, so it seemed to me. "Oh my God, get me out of here. The blood's running all over me." And it was coming nearer and nearer and it was mother underneath the couch, and it was my blood going on her hand. I was bleeding and hadn't been aware of it. I said to her "I'll go and find an air raid shelter."

The people next door were away and their air raid shelter wasn't being used. I went out into our yard and it was bloody levelled – just a heap of bloody bricks. I climbed over them and their shelter was alright but there was no door on it. The door had blown off. I told mother to stop there until I came back.

I walked down the entry. All the back walls had fallen down. I climbed over them all to Peel Road where I had a brother living over a butcher's shop. When I gets there he's got all his family and somebody else's family in their shelter. I told him that mother was alright and that I needed a dressing for my cut. "I'm going to St Leonard's Church, there's a dressing station there" I said. I left him to go back up and see mother. I went along Peel Road and when I got just past Grace Street – St Leonard's Church – the church was ablaze. No fire-engines in sight.

By the Cunard building, which is next to it, there was a fireman with a little wee pipe which was dribbling water. It struck me: "By Christ, this is the preparations they have!"

I said to the fireman "Get down off there. You're only acting the goat. What do you think that's going to do? The building's on fire!" The water was being pumped all the way from Akenside Street out of the Rimrose Brook. There was no water in the borough. They'd busted the mains at Strand Road, where the railway bridge is. The electricity comes across, the gas comes across there. They'd busted the lot.

I got back to mother's. We had no home, so I left with mother and we walked down to me sister's. When we got in we were filthy. They had no bath. I said "I'm going down to the beach to do my swillings." I got no dressing on the wounds. Salt water done it. There was no dressing stations. Grey Street was burnt out and St Leonard's was burnt out. All the emergency things were knocked out. A tent was put in the North Park where dockers, me and all the others, went for our dinner and tea-break. There was nothing on the docks. You couldn't work on the dock – only clearing up the debris, that's all.

The kind of shelter they built in the streets was built of

mortar and sand – lime and sand. They just fell down. They didn't need anything to blow them down. So we decided to get the women and children out of the town. This was before an air raid started. London had had it. Coventry had had it and Liverpool was the major port in the country. All the shipping, all the convoys, all mustered up from here. I went to the Town Clerk, because I wanted the women and kids out. He hadn't a clue, do you know that? He said "What are we going to convey them in?" "Jesus Christ," I said "the docks is loaded with meat wagons. They're going to do nothing if there's an air raid. Surely they can be commandeered." He didn't give no definite answer to my committee, the NUWM,[4] which was twelve men and twelve men who knew their stuff about the borough. We met and we agreed that we had to get the women and children out every night, out of danger. There would have been terrific casualties if we hadn't done that.

Liverpool Girl Where we were we had shelters. You got a lot of "This is my pitch. We were here last night." There was an awful lot of filth. There was a lot of scabies knocking around. You were that close together, everybody had it. No one ever looked clean. You had nowhere to wash – you had no time to wash. Unless you got things done first thing in the morning, that was your lot. There was no such thing as water in the shelters. You'd bring flasks of tea.

As a result of the raids I think people were more inclined to go to work. Absenteeism didn't go up. I think they were glad to get to work to forget the war. What could you do at home? Often your windows had gone or your roof had come off. You wouldn't want to sit in an empty house like that, would you?

In our area, what they used to do at night time, before it got dark people would climb on wagons and they'd go to the outskirts – anywhere – to get away from it, because it got that hot during the May Blitz. They'd stay there the night. They'd sleep in the lorry or often they'd just sit there, singing all night, and then they'd come back in the morning. Half the time you didn't know whether it was day or night.

Liverpool Mother Our Pat, she was born in the March, 1941, just before the May Blitz. I had her and the other little one would be two and a half and then the two boys. In our area we

didn't have any air raid shelters. They hadn't been built. We
didn't have a garden so we couldn't have an Anderson shelter.
We used to go underneath St George's Hall. I used to take the
four of them there. But it got too much to trek down there and
be half way when the sirens would go, so we started going
under a railway cutting.

**We used to go down steps and underneath the tunnel and take
turns in throwing bricks at the rats**

One hour on, one hour off. We had no lighting in the tunnel.
We were in darkness. One night we sheltered in Cain's
Brewery. It's Walkers & Tetley now. It was very handy for us so
we went there but a bomb dropped on it and the top was on fire
and we were underneath. We couldn't get out. There were 200
of us, children included. Luckily it was discovered that there
was an opening that led up another passageway, out into a
street at the other end, so we all managed to get out. But after
that the wardens came round and said it was compulsory
evacuation. If you didn't allow your children to go on their
own they'd be taken and you wouldn't know where they'd gone
to. A mother could go with them if she had children under five
years of age.

**People were worn down. I can honestly say Hitler would have got
the better of us – a couple more nights, there was no question
about it**

People were really scared. They were terrified. There were
ammunition ships in the dock at the time and the Germans
bombarded them and all day and all night there was explosions
where the ammunition were being blown up. And what wasn't
blowing up, our side was blowing up to save more damage.
There were explosions every minute. People's nerves were
really terrible.

The morning we were evacuated Lewis's, Blackler's, the
whole town was absolutely raging. It was alight. It was like
broad daylight in the early hours of the morning. Everything
was chaos. You were put on buses, lorries, anything at all, to

get you out to the safe areas. Whilst Liverpool was burning I was struggling to get on this bus and our Jimmy and our John had their bags of shrapnel in a little canvas bag tied round their necks, and they were arguing about their shrapnel and I was hammering them for to get on the bus. Apparently I'd given the wrong bag to each of them. The conductor said "Take a couple of pieces out of one and put it in the other and they'll be happy." We went to Southport.

They called us dirty evacuees, but we hadn't had water for 5 days before leaving, so you can't expect people to be clean

The only water we had was from the Mount. There was a spring there. We used to queue up for a bucket of water, and that had to do for everything. After a few days I had to come back from Southport to collect some clothes for the children. It was a job getting back because they'd bombed Bootle and you couldn't get a train through. When I eventually got home I found they'd looted it. They'd left the furniture, but they'd stripped the dishes and all my sheets and blankets. There was a lot of looting in Park Lane, Park Road. Human nature didn't change just because there was a war on.

I had a sister who lived in Southport and she said I could live in with her, but there wasn't the room – they had their two children and my mother and her mother-in-law. So she got me to go and stay with a lady. But I couldn't stay there – I had to be out by 9 o'clock in the morning and I wasn't allowed back until half past six at night. Through a minister of the Church I moved into a large house owned by one of the Hartleys, the jam people. Christina her name was. She'd bought this house and put beds and chest-of-drawers, and the rooms were let off to mothers and children, like bedsitters. There were six mothers and we had a communal kitchen. It was beautiful and clean and you had every facility for washing. She used to claim billeting allowance from the government for as many as she had in the house.

At Southport we lived like kings. I had the newborn baby, the little one of two and our John and Jimmy. They weren't big tea drinkers, but you still got a tea ration for your newborn baby and each child. Tea was like gold, so anybody who knew you had two quarters of tea – a pound of steak! Or a fowl! Bartering was going on. My children were as well dressed as any in Southport. You didn't pay for the clothes. You got all the cast-offs and you gave them clothing coupons. It was barter. They had the money, but if you had a few children you had the ration books and the clothing coupons. There was money in Southport.

Same as your sugar – you wouldn't be using all your ration, so they'd barter it for fruit. It was very, very hard to get fruit during the war, but they had it. They got it.

I went into a house in Oxford Road to do some cleaning for one of these WVS – I thought I was having a dream. You couldn't get in the cellar for food

It hadn't been bought during the war. It had been bought by the hundredweight before the war. She had everything that was on ration. Mind, she was very very good. You never came away empty handed. A bit of fruit for the children, or currants or something.

Royal Engineer When the raids were on in London my wife was evacuated down in . . . I think it was down in Norfolk. She went to this school which they had made into an evacuation centre and they loaded them on coaches and took them down to Norfolk. When they landed them in this place they unloaded them on the pavement. She had the two children, the two girls. The people who had already applied for them came along but this woman who my wife was supposed to go with, when she saw the two girls she said "Oh no, I don't want no children." And she was left there. Everybody was gone and she was sitting on the pavement in this village, crying, with the two kids. No one wanted to know. A young girl about her own age walked up and said "What's wrong? I'll take you home with me." She went and stopped with her for about three years. It just shows what it was like. They thought they was onto a good thing, some of them. They changed their minds afterwards.

London Girl I was working at Knight's, the soapworks, when we got bombed out. We was evacuated to Finchley. Mum and me. When we got to Finchley we knocked on the door of this house we were supposed to go to and we said "Can you take us in?" She said "You can come in, but we don't want you. We've got a corpse laying here." I says to our mum "I ain't going in there! I ain't going in there!" She didn't want us anyway. She was la-de-dah. We had no clothes with us. Nothing. As we was walking along – we was both crying – there was a woman standing at her gate and she saw us and she says "What's the matter?" So I said "That woman up there don't want us." So she said "You can come in here if you like." Whilst we were at Finchley dad got this house from the Council and he went and got the bits and pieces of furniture we had left, that was in storage, and we came here, to Gresham Road.

Her Mother When we came here the bombing started again and Rene said "Ooh, I can't stop here" and then we went to Oakham, Rutland.

Being us we got the worst of it. We was living in bleeding stables, mum and me

London Girl Going to Rutland wasn't the first time I'd seen country. We used to go to Southend, and I went hopping once when I had diptheria.

Her Mother No, she had bronchial pneumonia. We went with Lil Stephens.

London Girl When we lived in the stables we had no furniture. We was sleeping on hay. It was the summer. We used to go for walks down to Cottesmore aerodrome in the afternoon and we used to have our meals in the WVS. Then we got digs eventually, but mum decided to come home to dad. But me, I stopped down there and stayed with someone else. I worked in the picture house in Oakham. It was a nice picture house. It had a circle and everything. I knew a lot about the pictures because my dad worked in picture houses before the war. I was well in with everybody down there, but it seemed to me that they were calling a lot of people up, so I said to Mr Black, the manager "'Ere, Mr Black, it seems they aren't half calling people up. I

So I joined the Land Army.

---

[1] The first bombs to fall on Britain killed 25 sailors aboard cruisers on the Firth of Forth, 16 October 1939. The first civilian casualty of an air raid occurred at Bridge of Waith, Orkney, 16 March 1940. Cundy Road, Custom House, along with other East London dockland areas, did receive the first concentrated mainland bombing.

[2] Curiously, virtually all books state that the London Blitz started on a Saturday evening, 7 September 1940. But the East London *Stratford Express* in its report of 13 September 1940, states that the raids started on Friday evening, 6 September.

[3] 3–11 May 1941.

[4] National Unemployed Workers' Movement.

---

7 As long as your heart was ticking these doctors reckoned you were alright

Londoner I thought they wouldn't take me because of my age, and for medical reasons, and less than eight months later I'm on a boat going for a ride. I lived in Tottenham at the time. 1940 I got my medical, and I went in in 1941, January 2nd. I went to a sort of parish hall in Forster Street for the medical. They asked you "Have you had any illnesses?", what sort of health you was enjoying, or otherwise. "Alright, you'll hear from us, one way or another." And I thought "I hope to·Christ I don't."

Railwayman I was late. I dodged them for 18 months. I was working on the railway, up the Western Junction, back of Stratford station. When the air raids started they decided we would have to do night duty, standing on the railway for a shilling a night. We had to parade up and down, watching the bombs drop, which wasn't very nice at the beginning, because we were working on our own. This was on top of our 48 hours, because we had to work Saturdays. If you didn't work you didn't get paid. That shilling was handy though – seven bob a week.

I was on guard one night, walking up and down the railway, and there was a big raid on. All the lines had been blown up from previous raids – all your switch lines, so when the big mainline trains came through you had to get a crowbar and push the points through, put a clip on it underneath, screw it up so it held and then wave the train by. After he went you had to undo it and push it back again. This night a big air raid came over and there was a big express standing there, waiting for me to change the points. Next thing, a bomb dropped on Jenson and Nicholsons, the paint factory, and everywhere there was paint, like a rainbow. I dived under these sandbags and when I got up and looked the railway lines were standing vertical, and there was a big hole. The train's standing there, choo, choo, choo, still waiting, and the signal bloke's shouting out "Switch 'em over." So I said "Fuck 'em, you an' all" and I threw the crowbar, and I pissed off. It was alright for the signalman, he was sandbagged in his little box. They never saw me no more, the railway. That was my lot. I ran along the railway, got to Angel Lane and dived down the shelter. "What's the matter?" the wife said. "I've packed that lark up" I said. We went down to Norwich.

     After six months in Norfolk we came back to London and got a house in Woodford. I went over to Chingford, to the Labour Exchange, and they gave me a job on the dust – the dustmen, up Chingford Mount. It nearly killed me. I was there about three weeks when the foreman called me into the office and said "I've got your papers here. I can't exempt you. If you'd been here for three months you'd have been exempt occupation. I'm sorry," he said, "but they've caught up with you." I more or less give up then.

In this war, a lot of people didn't want to know. They didn't want their sons, their husbands to go

I knew two blokes who went on the run. They had relations at Maidstone. Straight away they was down there, and mixed in with the pikies, in with the gyppos and they lived off the land. They went fruit picking, hop picking, thieving – everything, right through the seasons, working on the farms, fiddling

"I had a wife and kiddie. I couldn't have gone on the run – they'd have stopped her allowance if I did."

about. They done alright out of it. I had a wife and kiddie. I couldn't have gone on the run – they'd have stopped her allowance if I did.

I thought to myself "Sod it. Might as well go." She kept saying to me "You want to go! You want to go! I know you want to go." I didn't want to go, but what could I do? I just dropped in with the rest. Done what you was told.

Car Worker I had two good mates. I regret it now, because of the money I wasted, but every night I used to go home, have a wash, put another shirt on, because we never had suits in them days even though you could get a suit for 50/-, but 50/- was a lot of money. I used to go the *Anglers* pub which is just past Fords every night, me and my two mates. Then we started getting up parties and going up Forest Gate skating rink – men and women together. We used to form up crocodiles and all this nonsense and get slung out. All we done then was try to enjoy ourselves. Although we didn't realise it, subconsciously we must have realised we were losing out with the threat of being called up any minute, and the fact you was working long hours in a factory.

40   I was registered with the first lot of 19's, but I was near enough 20 before I got called up. Briggs held us back. When we registered we didn't care. We wasn't bothered about work. I used to work in the wood mill at Briggs. The bloke I worked with, he was going in the airforce (incidentally, he never came back), and I was going in the airforce with him. Another bloke was going in the navy. The three of us used to work a machine where you held a jig together and you used to work it round. It was the inside panel of a door – the part where you wound the handle for the window to go up and down.

We were working away and we were singing. The foreman used to stand in an office, up the top, glaring down at you all day. If you went up the toilet and had a smoke he'd be up there after you – "Get the hell out of it." You've got to remember that it was a time where if you had a job you looked after it, 'cos you was glad of the fact you was in work.

But now that we were registered things were different. As I say, we were singing and he come down and he said "You can't sing and work at the same time." Sò I said "Why? We deafening yer? These machines are making more noise than we are." "If I have any more out of you," he said "you'll be out the gate." That same day I went home and my mother was looking out the bedroom window. She said "Your papers have come." I shot indoors and I got hold of 'em. I went back next morning. I went up the office. "You know what you can do with your job now, don't you?"

This might sound strange, but there was glamour in going into the services, in some ways. Your mates used to come home from the army on leave. They used to go in the pub and everybody used to look at 'em. They were "One of our soldiers. One of our boys." They'd take no notice of you. You were only a common civvie, and gradually it got through to you that you wanted to be like that. But you didn't get any inclination what you was letting yourself in for because when you drew your first weeks pay, ten bob they slung in your hand. "Christ" you thought, "I've got to buy writing paper, envelopes, stamps, fags, everything out of this." Ten bob didn't last five minutes. **Glaswegian** I joined the RAF because I didn't want to go in the Corps of Signals. It would be just like the Post Office all over again. Because I was a Post Office engineer it was automatic that I would get channelled into the Corps of Signals. The only thing they'd release you for was aircraft or submarines.

Londoner I volunteered to get in what I wanted to get in – that was the RASC.[1] I went to Romford to volunteer. At that time I was deputy manager of Sainsburys at Ilford. I'd been out as relief manager when the manager went on holiday. I was a bit of a naughty boy because I got ticked off for volunteering by Sainsburys. The food trade was a sort of semi-priority trade. Those sort of people didn't go in until late. They went in around '41, '42. When I joined up I went to Manchester on a 12 week course. I'm a qualified mechanic – supposed to be. That's what I joined up to be, but when I got posted to Africa I didn't want to know. That's why I became a Company Sergeant Major. The heat was so bad. You couldn't touch a lorry. It was red hot.

Essex Lad I was working at Crompton-Parkinsons at Chelmsford when I had to register for National Service. Eighteen I suppose I must have been. In my own mind I was going in the RAF, come what may. I always wanted to go in the airforce. I was dead keen on the airforce long before the war, because I was interested in aircraft. I used to go to the Hendon air displays and I used to keep scrapbooks of aircraft. The war for me was a means of getting into the airforce to fly.

Very few aircrew that I met ever confessed to being aircrew for patriotic reasons

It was a means of getting into the airforce and to fly. I met lots of people like myself. Also, it meant more money, rank on their arms and a decent uniform.

Miner I was working in Yorkshire. I worked at South Kirkby. It's about ten miles from Doncaster. I volunteered to get out the pit. I volunteered for the Merchant Navy. You had to go to Barnsley before the Tribunal. They made me exempt. I couldn't leave the pit. You got papers to say you was exempt. I felt a bit sore about it at the time. There was some miners that had volunteered before me and had went into the services and they was called back, but those that had gone abroad when the

". . . it meant more money, rank on their arms and a decent uniform."

war first kicked off, they was out of it. It was Bevin[2] who came in and stopped it. I worked with a lot of lads who were re-directed down the mines.

Oxford Lad Early '41 I volunteered. I volunteered because I wanted to help the war effort and fight fascism. I was only young. You went to a place in St Michael's Street for the medical. As long as your heart was ticking these doctors reckoned you were alright. I did have something wrong with my spine, due to an accident in the past, but I was still accepted. I went to Cardington as a ground gunner in the airforce.

The basic training was pretty rough. I was one of the first lot to be made into a RAF regiment, which was 208 Squadron. You had a lot of army officers who were transferred into the RAF regiment. You had heavy boots and a set of khaki denims, and one suit of blue. The khaki stuff smelt terrible. It was awful. It was all spit and polish. I had trouble with my feet and I couldn't wear these army boots. I went sick with it. I went down the sick bay and the NCO would come in and he'd think everyone was malingering and he'd have all the windows open, in the middle of winter, and they'd have you parade outside to wake you up. In the end I wanted to get away. I got worse, you see – things like a route march, with my legs and feet. I couldn't go any further. I just dropped out. They used to try and put me on a charge of malingering. It was terrible.

Glaswegian Lad I joined the army to fight fascism. '41 I went in. As a young person I was very romantic. I seen things in black and white terms. I didn't think I had much freedom in civvy street, but I thought what I had was worth fighting for. So I go into the military thinking we've got a crusading crowd of people here who are even more aware than the civilian – that he's prepared to get a gun and go and fight for that guy. And then to find that this guy knows less about freedom than what I'd come from, and that anything I had been taught about the baddie and the Nazi and the fascists was plonk there in front of me, in this crowd of people who were supposed to be enlightened, informed and geared up to fight it. So how the hell do you move from that square to the enemy? When you find the enemy's in your midst?

I got arrested six months after I was in for something I didnae do. They stuck me in a wee oven-like place and kept me in there. They gave me 12 days Field Punishment No. 1

In they days it meant that you pack all your kit, every piece, fill your water bottle and then they double you up and down for an hour with your rifle until you're dropping. I done it twice. I began to think about it. "What the bloody hell am I doing this for? This is stupid." But the thing I did notice was that everybody else was seeming to do it in their stride, and I was finding it difficult. I was prepared to accept that the army must have discipline, and that sometimes they can make mistakes like everybody else, so I said "Alright Walter, you're a soldier, you've got to do this, along with the rest." But then I thought "This is no right. I'm no guilty. I shouldnae being doing this" and I stopped and took all my stuff off, put it on the thingme and sat on it. "That's me finished" I said, "I don't deserve this."

I don't think I even got to my feet – two guys whipped me the way I was, into jail. Two things I discovered was that the rest of the guys were dead fly. They didnae have water in their water bottles and they packed bits of paper in their packs. I was

44   running about with my pack and my waterbottle full because I thought I had to do it the military way. I thought this is what you've got to do to beat this guy Hitler. How naive can you get?

The first time I ever went absent was at that time. I was at Mossbank. I lost my remission there, for trying to escape, because I let my diet tin drop on the floor. I was unsure, you know? – because I didnae know what it was all about. You'd to run and grab your diet. All the rest of them were good at it, but I dropped mine all over the floor and it ran all over this staff's feet and I made a dive after it. "Catch him! He's trying to escape!" That's a fact. Into the cells right away. Locked up. Bread and water. Taken up in front of the commanding officer. I thought "Och, I'll give an explanation" – "I was trying to do this sir – " and a guy's stood at the back of me with a big pacing stick, digging it in my back everytime I spoke. I just turned round and Bang! I belted him. And that was me finished. That was it all starting. The whole situation changed. I said "This army's no what I thought it was." I just folded up my sleeves and said "Right, there's two wars here. Let's get intae it."

---

[1] Royal Army Service Corps.
[2] Ernest Bevin, Minister of Labour.

---

8 Sometimes you sit down and you say "What the hell am I doing here? There's no war in our country"

Jamaican I was living in Kingston, Water Street, when I joined up. I was still going to school. A friend of mine and me, we set out one morning to go to school and we had to pass the recruiting place. There was a queue of lads standing outside – high school lads. The place wasn't open yet. My friend, he said "What about we go join the airforce?" I said "Oh no, your mudder will kill you if she hear you join the airforce" for there

was only one kid in that family and the mother and father
worked – the father was a tramcar driver and every penny that
he earns he spend on this lad. But anyway, we plucked up the
courage and we went in and we joined. I was 17.

I had no idea what I was going to be when I was at school.
My uncle was a joiner – what we call carpenter, back home. I
used to be with him all the while – every spare time that I get I
always with him. I picked up a lot of work off him. He said
"Alright, if you want to leave school you can come with me as
an apprentice." The work situation wasn't too good. Things
were cheap but the unemployment and the work was very
appalling. Most of the work was in the plantations – sugar. For
tradesmen the money was very very good, but for ordinary
labourers the pay was very bad. Joining the airforce was
something I did on the spur of the moment.

After we joined, the hardest part was when he come back for
he had to tell his mother that he joined the airforce. It was a
row. I didn't tell anybody. My mother was living in St Ann's.
She found out eventually, when I was on my way to England. I
don't think she was upset, for actually I didn't grow up with my
parents. I grow up on my own. I went away to Montego Bay
when I was about eight or nine. I was living with my sister at the
time I joined the airforce.

When the card came for me to report to camp, I didn't. I
decided to change my mind. At this time the Americans were
building a camp at a place called Sandy Gully. It was
swampland. America said to Britain "You can have all the
material you want, but you won't get one man from America to
fight for you." This was at the beginning of the war. America
was supplying Britain with all the material that they wanted
and they didn't see any way in which Britain could pay for it, so
they said "We'll lease the West Indian islands off you –
Jamaica, Trinidad."

It didn't cause any bad feeling with us for actually it
provided work for thousands and thousands. When the
Americans came here and started to build the base the pay was
so great, they would have been glad if they'd built the base all
over the whole island! If I remember rightly, when the
Americans started the base Churchill told Roosevelt not to pay

the amount of money they were paying to the Jamaican worker, for after they finished there would be no more work and they'd be looking for the same pay. But the Americans said they wanted the job doing and as long as the man can do the job, he got paid for it.

It was because of the fantastic money that they were paying that I was having second thoughts about joining the airforce. After I received the card saying I should report to camp three days passed and then a Landrover[1] pulled up. It was morning. I was just getting up and I come out onto the steps. There was police and an army corporal. They said "Mr Campbell in?" I nearly said 'Yes", but I realised what was going on. I told them he was away. They said "When you see him, just tell him he's to report at the camp."

The camp was at Port Royal. I went to the camp with two pairs of shoes, for in Jamaica you scarcely see a bloke with just a one-colour pair of shoes. His shoes either black and white or brown and white. You can just imagine six or seven hundred people on the barrack square drilling, and all of them have different shoes on – and different pants, for there was no uniform at all. One of my pairs was black and white, and one brown and white, for we scarcely in those days go in a shop and buy a pair of shoes.

In a fortnight, after all this drilling, I had no shoes at all, except the uppers. Some of us used wires and tied them on. Finally we got the uniform. The boat that was originally coming with the uniform was sunk. A second boat came, but there wasn't enough uniform to go round. I just had pants – no tunic to fit, you see. In a couple of days another boat came in and we all got fixed up.

There was a lot of shipping getting knocked off in the Atlantic round the West Indies. The Germans used to have submarines waiting – as soon as they see a ship – it's gone! The fishermen, they were coming in every morning with barrels of salt fish and all different kinds of provisions from these sunk ships. A lot of lads got scared and wouldn't join up. It was either the first or the second batch of men to leave Jamaica for the airforce, that their boat was sunk. They never made the Atlantic. We all got scared then.

As soon as we were properly fixed up with uniform we was on a 36 hour pass, for we were going away on the Monday. The news got out somehow or another, because they were trying to keep it secret. It was very hush-hush, because the news was getting out and these boats were going down. It was dark when we left. The boat, the *SS Cuba*, come in. We came by launch across the sea to the boat. When we looked back the pier was full of people come to say farewell. We arrived in Britain in the winter.

We arrived in Greenock in the night. The whole place was in darkness. We couldn't make out anything at all. Even the train was in darkness – just this little light with the long shade. When we got on the train there was only the Salvation Army. They was there giving us cups of tea and cake. That's all you could see – just a hand coming through the window. I looked out the window after the train set out – there wasn't much to see. I turned to another lad. I said "Where the hell are we going? Can you see anything of houses, or anything?" He said "No." Then we start to make out shapes. I said "I can't see anything here – all I can see is blessed factories." Which was houses! For seeing chimneys on houses, that is something we don't have back home. In the early hours of the morning we reached Filey, which was our destination. We spent about ten weeks there, then I went to Henlow, and then I came back to Filey for a while. I was with the third batch of lads that came over. I was trained for air-gunner. Most of the time I was on stand-by.

It was about thirty shillings a week I was getting when I joined the airforce, I think. Once we leave Jamaica, the Jamaican government was paying five shillings a week more to the Jamaican airman, on top of the RAF pay. We used to get extra sugar. I adapt quickly to tea without sugar, or just a little bit, but a lot couldn't. The thing we couldn't adapt to very quick was this heap of spuds. We didn't like it. In some camps we had our own cooks.

When we first arrived they tried to make an effort. As I say, the tea had no sugar in, as everything was on ration, but as a lot couldn't drink it, so we used to get an extra ration of sugar. On the West Indian table there's always extra sugar. We used to have all the English trying to get on the West Indian table. They

"At times I thought 'Why on earth did you volunteer?'"

were always there. We got extra tropical food. Some camps you go there was older men that have been to the tropic countries and they like the tropic food, so when they see it on the West Indian table they want to get onto that table too. At first the extra sugar caused a bit of resentment. When they understand that all this extra sugar was being paid for by the Jamaican government they then said it was a different matter. They believed we were getting extras, that they were getting privileges.

At times I thought "Why on earth did you volunteer?" Especially when we had to go around Filey, on these ack-ack guns for target practice. It was always early in the morning. The plane would be up there with the target on. You're shooting at this plane at 6 o'clock in the morning. It was always early in the morning. Winter, summer, autumn, you're at it. Sometimes you sit down and you say "What the hell am I doing here? There's no war in our country."

---

[1] Landrovers went into production in 1947. Obviously a reference to a similar type of vehicle.

---

9 He went out one morning and he didn't come home for over three years

---

London Woman My husband went in the navy. After his basic training he had a very short leave – ten days, I think. He said he

was going abroad. I went back with him to Portsmouth –
Southsea – and I got lodgings for one or two nights. And then
he went off. He went out one morning and he didn't come back
for three years.

Mechanic Our convoy out was about 50 ships. We knew where
we were going when they issued us these pith helmets on the
ship, when we were half way there. They also gave us our
tropical kit. The pith helmet was plain on top and you had to
have a band – terrific yards of this sort of yellow material which
you had to keep winding and winding and winding. There was
a certain way you had to do it, to get all the pleats in it. We was
all shown how to do it, but none of us could do it. Only the old
soldiers could do it, and when you wanted yours done, it was
ten bob a time they were charging. Oh shocking! All the old
soldiers were promoted as soon as war broke out and they were
the biggest fiddlers under the sun. Going out we stopped at'
Durban for two weeks. That's when I first felt the sun. It was
red hot.

Commercial Traveller I was an electrician in the airforce.
When I passed out they stationed me at 41 MU at Slough and I
went out with a Waaf. I got the wrong side of her and the next
thing I knew I got posted. She was in the posting office, the
bloody cow! I didn't know where I was going. Just told us we
were going overseas.

They took us out in the middle of the night. A train stopped
in the middle of nowhere. We went on this bleeding train, you
didn't know how long you was going to be. It went and it
moved and it kept on going and going. You didn't know when
it was going to stop, where it was going to stop. Finally, we got
some place. One of the blokes told us we were there. We were in
bloody Greenock! Fancy taking us all the way to Greenock to
go to bleeding Gibraltar, though at the time we still didn't
know where we was going. I was absolutely whacked. I'd been
on the train for 15 hours. The worst part was not knowing
where it was going. If you ever had the feeling of being treated
like cannon fodder, that was it. We got on the boat and we still
didn't know where we were going.

They took us down below, below the hold. You had all your
benches where you used to eat and above that they gave you a

hammock. You had to sling your hammock up. Rows and rows of hammocks. All of a sudden you could hear the engines chugging. You was going somewhere, but you didn't bloody well know where. You didn't know where it was until you landed. Throughout the journey you heard Boom, Boom – bloody depth charges going. All night long. You could feel it vibrating through the whole boat.

I used to feel seasick. In the daytime you used to sit at the benches, where you ate, with your hammock swinging above you. You realised you were going somewhere warmer because it was getting stifling down in the ship. And then, all of a sudden, my hammock snapped. Bang! They took me to the hospital ward and I played it up a bit. I had a couple of nice cushy days there. I also earned a bit of money. I was a tailor by trade and all the sergeants gave me their stripes to sew on. I got a bit of drop that way.

Eventually we landed and we could see. We were in Gibraltar. Was it baking! They took us to this place, which was the North Front Aerodrome (before the war it was a race-course). There was nothing there. They didn't expect us. They had two bases at Gibraltar. One was the seaplane base and this was the land base. They had nowhere for us to sleep. They had loads of petrol cans so they gave us six petrol cans, they gave us three biscuits and a couple of blankets. And that's how we had to sleep for nearly three months. You just wasn't used to it.

They gave you a tin plate and you went into the cookhouse and after you washed it in a thing like a horse trough. You had to be very careful with water. There was so little of it. You had to wash in sea water. And as you sat there – bleeding flies. As fast as you swatted them they were on you again – Oh, it was the most horrifying experience. Flies galore on every bleeding thing. The most unsanitary conditions. And as I say, you had to sleep out in the open. The officers? Where were they? Oh, they had quarters. Definitely. The Morocco Hotel. Oh yes.

10

My mother simply said to me "I didn't give birth to you to have you killed at the age of 23 so good luck to you"

Commercial Artist I was 23 when the war broke out. I was a ripe age for it. I was extraordinarily lucky because I had a whole set of lucky circumstances which led me to take my position against the war. It went back before the war.

I had an ordinary kind of education at an elementary school and secondary school in Forest Gate, London. I then went onto art school at the West Ham Tech and it was there that my education in thinking began to develop. There wasn't much political thought going on but we began to think about Life, with a capital "L", and getting into all that sort of thing. There was a young feller there who was, in fact, black and he was the only black boy in the school. He got very interested in politics and became a pacifist. He started me thinking and started us all discussing it. We had a little group of four who were very close friends. We used to go everywhere together, do everything together.

At the time of the Munich crisis I was thinking "Oh God, I should go into the Home Guard"[1] or do something – prepare myself for what was obviously coming. In the intervening year, by the time war broke out, three out of the four of us had become conscientious objectors. We all split up in different directions and my lucky chance grew out of the fact that in June 1939 I'd gone for a holiday in the country – down in Sussex – and had fallen in love with a farmer's daughter. Fortunately she reciprocated and so when it all happened in September '39 she said "Come down here." She had a caravan ready for me to go to, so I went and lived down on the farm. I lost my job. I was sacked a week before war broke out.

The farm was at Cowden, near Edenbridge. My parents were, I think, a little shocked that I had decided to be a conscientious objector. My father had just been too old for the First World War. He may have well swung the lead a bit – I don't know. He was self-employed and I think he just about kept himself out of it by virtue of having his little woodworking business to keep going. So he had no great feelings about it. My mother simply said to me "I didn't give birth to you to have you killed at the age of 23, so good luck to you." In the event, later on, she turned out to be quite a support in that sort of way.

I started doing odd jobs for the farmer and got into farmwork. I saw an advertisement for training for tractor drivers in the Kent War Agricultural Committee. I went over to Maidstone and did a fortnight's course in tractor driving and after that I was able to be offered jobs as a skilled agricultural worker. By this time my age group had come up and I had registered as a conscientious objector. I went and lived on two or three farms out in Kent, in the Sheppey area, driving tractors. I became, I think I can say, a skilled tractor driver. They actually trusted me with one of the first yellow Caterpillars in the country, when they began to come over on Lend-Lease from America. I was very proudly going up and down with a four-furrow plough, harrowing and cultivating and doing all that bit.

Farms in those days had a lot of people working on them, not like now where you can get hundreds and hundreds of acres run by six men with machines. They still had horses. My big tractor was the first one to be introduced. The guy who got it eventually became Sheriff of Kent. Man called Doubleday. He got a knighthood for his services, of ploughing up hundreds of acres of marshland, getting £2 an acre subsidy, just for getting me to work on it for him.

There was a lot of people working on the farm. There were about 20 men lining up at ten past six in the morning. They were exempted. Most of them would have been of military age. I'm sure there were quite a few of them that were bloody glad they were exempted. There was no patriotic talk.

In the meantime I had been called up for the Tribunal. I was turned down

I had no history of having belonged to either a religious body or political group which had a recognised position that they would accept. My objection was based on my wishy-washy humanitarian, pacifist, aesthetic objections. An "artist" you know – can't have anything to do with this . . . This didn't go down very well! I was turned down also at the Appeal. The Labour Exchange then approached me and they said "We understand this is your position – would you be prepared to go into the Fire Service?" I thought around that for a couple of days and said "OK, I will accept the Fire Service."

I submitted myself for a medical examination which if you're going in the forces is the crucial thing you must never do. Once you've been through a medical they reckon they've got you. I went through the medical on the strict understanding (I signed a thing) that it was the Fire Service, and stood back, expecting to be called up. By this time it was after 1941. The Blitz had come and gone and there just wasn't a demand for firemen any more. I was never called up.

At work I kept my beliefs to myself. It never arose. I'd got married in the meantime, though not to the farmer's daughter. My wife's family knew. The brother-in-law was a bit hostile. He wasn't in the army, but he was in the Home Guard and was as patriotic as all people are who are not doing very much. My brother was very hostile too, until he got called up.

He was a lot older than me and he'd worked in an insurance office all his life. Going to and from Rickmansworth, where he lived, to the City of London. He was called up and drafted first to Kettering, where he had a hell of a time. He told me afterwards he very nearly deserted because it was so rough. He managed to get himself in the Pay Corps and lived at home. Going from Rickmansworth to the City on a train an hour earlier than the one he used to go up to the office before. He flirted with the British Union of Fascists before the war and was a bit patriotic. He was very ashamed of me in the first instance.

After we got married we got fed up where we were and we moved back to London and I got a job as a gardener/handyman. An old friend of mine had been off to Scotland, on the Forestry. Up there there was much more of a group of conchies working together. They had a lot more discussion and the whole thing was getting politicised. He'd got onto Herbert

54   Read's[2] writings, which was a contact between us as art students and radical ideas. He introduced me to *Poetry and Anarchism* and then the *Philosophy of Anarchism*. These both turned me on. And from there I just made the trek up to Belsize Road, which was where the Freedom Press office was in those days. I introduced myself and started going to their meetings. It was three and a half years of the war before I worked around from wishy-washy, simple personal opposition to the war to sewing all these things together in terms of what I now see as the pointlessness of objecting to war without objecting to the state which depends upon war.

Tramp I was in Ipswich casual ward the day war broke out. I sensed that this was an end of an era, that the whole thing was coming to an end. Most of the casual wards were closed down because they were wanted, to be used either as additional hospital accomodation or as ARP centres. I suppose, also, the authorities thought there would no longer be any need to provide accomodation for dossers, but all through the war years there were still people on the road – not so many, but certainly a certain number.

I had decided to be a conscientious objector. In 1939 when I should have registered for military service I didn't go. I'd made up my mind I wasn't going to register, and that I was going to go to prison, but people in the movement talked to me about this and said it was rather silly going to prison – you can't achieve anything in jail. Several months after I should have registered I came to the conclusion they were right, so long as the country allowed you to do anti-war activity. I have a great respect for those conscientious objectors who did go to prison though. They stood their ground, the absolutists, and I think they were very wonderful and very brave people.

Detention Centre Inmate The most interesting group in the Detention Centre, for me. were the conscientious objectors. They were separated from us by the authorities. Unlike us they were kept in single cells and of course, they wouldn't do the military training, which was the main programme for most of the inmates.

When you registered the normal procedure was the following: if you had a long record to which you could point as a pacifist in civilian life, and all the evidence was produced at court, you could be registered as a pacifist or for non-combatant duties. But most people who decided to be conscientious objectors never had any record to prove it. A large proportion of these people could not be registered by the Tribunals as conscientious objectors, and they were therefore liable for call up. If they refused to submit, and refused to put the uniform on, it was an automatic six months.

What they did was, they used to bring them in, put them in a cell, strip them naked, throw a uniform in, and that's it. You put it on or you don't, and in the middle of winter that's no joke. To reinforce the point, like as not they'd put a hose on him, wet the whole bloody place out, including the uniform. Every pressure was used, but some of these people were incredibly hard. OK – some of them would eventually submit and put the uniform on, but made it clear that they were only wearing it as clothing, and not as a mark of acceptance. They weren't stupid. They knew in the first few months there was no point in making life too difficult.

At the end of the six months they would come up again and if they still refused it would be another six months. But they got to know that the third time, possibly the fourth time, the authorities would finally give in, and register them. All of the ones I came across knew this procedure. They were prepared to suffer 18 months rather than submit to being called up. To reinforce their position vis a vis their statement that they were conscientious objectors they used to play up rough a month before the end of their sentence, so as to have evidence to show that they were sincere.

---

[1] The Home Guard was created after the war started. This is obviously a slip for ARP (Air Raid Precautions).
[2] Art historian and critic, poet and anarchist.

11

The first time I came home I had me great big haversack, me gas mask and me tin helmet and me mum looked at me and said "Ooh Rene, whatever have they done to yer?"

London Girl All women under 40[1] had to do some sort of war work. We all had to fill a form in – how old we was, whether we wanted to go in munitions or whether we wanted to go in the airforce or in the Land Army, and so on. I just put down the airforce. I didn't think nothing was going to come of the war, and then it happened – I got called up. This was when I was at Rutland, working in the picture house.

I joined the Land Army to try and get out of it. I was going to drive this horse and milk cart. I was frightened of the bleeding horse. I was shit scared, but I was going to have a go. I'd rather do that than get called up. I told them "I can't go in the airforce now, I've joined the Land Army." But they said "You'll have to take your Land Army clothes back. You've got to go in the airforce." I was called up two days before Christmas. I had to go to Gloucester and then I went to Morecambe for me training. We used to march along the front in the wind.

I'll never forget the first time I came home. I had thick grey stockings on, and your heavy shoes and your hat – you don't know how to do nothing, press your uniform or nothing. You're a sort of sprog, int yer? I had me great big haversack with me gasmask and me tin helmet and me mum looked at me and said "Ooh Rene, whatever have they done to yer?"

London Clippie If you weren't married (I was doing machining – needlework) and it wasn't considered essential you had to go away to work, in ammunitions or something like that. I didn't want to go in ammunitions because I didn't want to go away. So I went on the buses as a conductress. I was in the first ladies that went on the buses. It was 1940. There were woman conductors but not one woman driver. The younger men on the

"I had thick grey stockings on, and your heavy shoes and your hat."

buses had been taken for the services. We were only replacing them. The drivers were usually older men.

We had to have very stringent medical tests before they would allow us in. We had a week out with the conductor, and then we were left to our own mercies. I did the 25 route which was Becontree Heath to Victoria; through Oxford Street, Bond Street. I also did the 40 route which was from Wanstead round to Camberwell Green. We used to get well-known people on the buses a lot, especially round Bond Street and Piccadilly. The reason was that they couldn't get the petrol to run their cars. I enjoyed the comradeship – being on the same route every day you met the same people every day and you got to know them. You got some people who were awkward, like you always get. The day after we got the telegram about Dick, my brother, being killed someone on the bus said to me "Don't you know there's a war on?" I thought "I could tell you I know there's a war on." But the majority, there was a wonderful comradeship.

The people were remarkable. They weren't after the war was over. After the war was over and peace was declared, they weren't the same. We were taking the jobs away from men. I was financially better off on the buses than on machining. The Rag Trade never has been good pay. When you went on the buses you got a man's wages. I was quite comfortably off. And you got a free uniform and a travel pass.

West Country Girl I took what was then called School Certificate, and I got 8 credits. It was then a question of what I was going to do. There was an advertisement in the papers wanting girls to do radiolocation in the ATS. That was radar – radiolocation. My parents thought that would be quite a good career for me. I went to Axbridge to volunteer. My mother came with me. It got me away from the village. The war gave a lot of women opportunities they'd never had before. To join up and get away from service, for instance.

Yorkshire Girl My dad played hell with me – he's dead and gone now – but I went in service and I had no life at all. He took every penny off me I earned. I was more or less grafting for nothing. He used to say to this here lady where I was in service (this was in Thornton, Yorkshire) – he used to say "Take so much out for her clothes, and that's it." No pocket money. What good was that? Having to go to church with these flaming high society people. Every other Sunday I got off, and you either had all morning off and go to church in evening or we had morning church service and the evening off. Bloody hell. We grafted there for what? Nothing. Not much bloody fun it wasn't – black-leading grates and one thing and another. It was living-in there.

And then he got me a job in a pub, right on top, and he got my bike and used it, and I had to bus it. And when he came in pub and had a few drinks he carried on. Sometimes I was so scared of going home and getting a belting I used to have a spare key for me dad's allotment. I've slept in there with the chickens, on the haystack – anywhere, till I found out he'd gone out. One morning I thought he'd gone out and I crawled through the pantry window. Oh, did he leather me. He wouldn't just leather you. He'd tie you to a damn post and leather you.

I got my name down for the Land Army, and that was it. I was away. I worked near our kid where she was ATSing at Seaton. To look at you, you looked like bloody scouts. You had one of these flaming big hats on and breeches and boots. I'd helped my dad on his allotment, but I'd never done farmwork before. They had cattle and pigs. We did a bit of all sorts. I was in digs, in Nissen huts. The girls were from all over.

2nd London Girl I'd been evacuated but I came home and started work at 15. I went into various office jobs. In one I was very unhappy and I had to fight them to get out of it. You just couldn't leave your job like that. You had to go before a Tribunal. You had to have a very good reason for leaving your job. In this particular office the boss was a horrible swine. I

managed to win that case. The next job I went to I wanted to get
out of, so I pretended I had TB. My sister phoned up.

I think a lot of women were able to get out of war work by pretending they were ill. Getting a doctor's note

There was a certain amount of strictness though. My sister had impetigo – impetigo was rampant during the war. She had to come home, and the police came knocking because she had exceeded her time, her doctor's certificate.

Liverpool Girl I worked at Littlewoods. We were making what we called sleeves – wind sleeves for aerodromes. There was hundreds of sewing machines. You couldn't hear nothing. The hours were staggered. You'd do four nights on, two nights off, four nights on. Sometimes you got two wage packets in the one week. That was smashing when it fell like that. But after a while I couldn't stick it any longer. When I wanted to leave Littlewoods I had to go before a Tribunal. The Tribunal was in Leece Street. I was frightened about going before them. There was a couple of women and a few men behind a big table. The thought of facing them made me ill. I was on my own. Nobody else was allowed in. I was shaking more with fright than with sickness.

I told them that I couldn't stick it, that I wasn't well. They said "We don't think you could stick any work." But I was really ill, with lack of sleep and food was horrible to get. They said to me "You'll have to go on munitions or something else, but you're not fit for heavy work." The main thing was that they said I was only fit for light work. Ooh, was I glad! I run down them steps.

I went to work for Rootes, in their aircraft factory. I think they were making De Havilland Mosquitos. To be quite truthful I don't remember doing anything there. The hardest job I had was hiding away from the bosses. I was paid for nothing. I can picture to this day sitting under one of these aeroplanes. I didn't care if they gave me the sack, but they wouldn't let me go. I didn't want the job. But in the end they said the job was too heavy. A friend of mine worked on the railway, and that was what I was after. We were about £5 or £6

60 at Rootes, and I went onto twenty-four bob. It was no cop job. But you had a good laugh.

I got up at 4 o'clock in the morning. There were no buses. I walked. I lived in Lodge Lane. That was about $2\frac{1}{2}$ miles every morning. I was at Liverpool Central. They were strict about timekeeping, but if you were late you could always dodge in.

We used to empty all the fruit trains, first thing. Well, you never went short. The things that went on, it was laughable

There was one woman worked with us – Janie – she was deaf. In the summer maybe strawberries came in. We couldn't afford strawberries – in fact you couldn't get them. Or tomatoes would come in, and they were so dear. The foreman in charge of the women used to watch us. In fact, he could search us if he wanted to. But Janie was cute. We all used to take our coats to work, but she used to carry hers around with her. We weren't allowed to have pockets, but she used to tie a piece of string round the two sleeves of her coat and she'd stuff them with all kinds – tomatoes – oh, everything. She'd throw her coat over her arm and carry them out.

There was one time she put tomatoes down her chest. She didn't have her coat with her. And the railway policeman, Bill Hughes, he wasn't a bad feller, he had his job to do, he went over to her and put his arms around her waist and worked up to her chest and he squeezed her! He came up to us afterwards and said he knew she had the tomatoes. He said "It was the only way I could get my own back."

There was never any fear of me going into the forces as working on the railway was considered essential work. I wouldn't have gone in the forces – I'd have emigrated to Ireland before I'd have gone in. And I wouldn't have gone on them munitions. The danger of it.

Lancashire Woman I volunteered for the ROF[2] at Chorley. I volunteered to get some money. It was about the middle of the war. It was after I came to live in Leyland. I got friendly with some girls that worked there and I went along for a job. We didn't have no training, except somebody said "You do this" and that was it. You were left to it, on your own. I was on some

detonators that was all yellow. They were little things. They
went into a box and you had to check 'em. You had to see they
was level on top and smooth and if they weren't you had to
reject them. You could tell where these people worked because
they just looked like Chinese – yellow faces. It's like a sulphur
looking colour, this powder.

On another section it was all danger. They got more money
on that side. I worked there a bit. Somebody would say to you
"You're on that section today." It was doing the same work,
but it was more dangerous powder. It was black. You were in
little rooms and there were machines and stools. They used to
fill the detonators with this black stuff, and if it was too full
they used to rub it down a bit. They weren't supposed to, 'cos
that's dangerous, rubbing that. There was a lot of stuff wasted,
not done right. The folk weren't bothered.

There was a few explosions. Not very big ones. It was when
they were filling these shells. Sometimes they blew up. I don't
think anybody got killed while I was there. I was there 12
months. They did have accidents, but people didn't bother
about the danger. You were going to work and earning good
money.

You had to clock in when you went in. There were thousands
of cards. You got people clocking other people in. They used to
pick you out and search you when you were going in, as well, to
see if you'd got anything in your bag. You couldn't take
cigarettes or matches in. You weren't supposed to, but they
used to. They wangled it some way. They gave you overalls
when you went in. You had to take everything off – all your
outdoor clothes, shoes – I think it was because you hadn't to
take dirt in. When you got inside the factory you had to walk to
your section, and sometimes it was a long way. Perhaps a
couple of miles. It was a really big place.

They did nights. It was more money on nights. About £12 I
got for nights. We used to think it was a lot of money to have
£12! On nights they used to say there was a lot of carrying on
with blokes, with girls. There was a lot of carrying on at
Euxton. They'd say "Oh, you work at Euxton?" and give you
the eye. A lot of men and women worked there because of the
money. People travelled from everywhere to work there.

Blackpool, Liverpool, Manchester. There were special buses for some people. We used to have to fly for these buses to catch them at night going home. There used to be thousands going out at night.

I left before the war ended. I can't remember why I left, unless it was home duties. Looking after a kid. You can't do it the same on nights, can you? I wasn't working before the war. I never went out to work. That was the first time I was working. It was a bit strange, to go out to work and to go into a factory. You do feel as if you've earnt a bit of something. You don't feel so dependent for your money. I bought a new carpet while I was earning that money.

I thought the countryside was the idyllic scene. I painted pretty little farmyards. They used to get stuck on the walls in the artroom

Glasgow Girl I decided to join the Land Army and thereupon my dream was utterly shattered. I went to their recruiting office, which if I remember rightly was in Hope Street. I'd been working as a tracer in a draughtsman's office and I saw this as my chance to get away.

The Land Army sent me to the ———— at Dumbarton, about two miles from where I lived. They had an accredited herd. It was a beautifully run herd. But do you know why they engaged me? His wife was expecting a second child and they wanted me to cook, scrub the floor and do everything. She had a nurse who had been her childhood nurse, whom she'd had for the first child, and she was going to have her for the second child. This nurse was an old harridan. She expected all her orders to be carried out. I beefed. I told them I wasn't going to do it. I'd signed on for three years of agricultural work and I was shoved into this farm as a domestic. I got the boot from there. I was sent to ————, which was a hand milking farm.

It was difficult because there again they couldn't understand that I didn't want to do domestic work. I wanted to learn about work on a farm. Another girl working there was luckier than me. She was a great big girl and she made a boyfriend of the first ploughman and that was one up for her because she learnt

a lot from this wee guy. It was the strangest business. This huge,
huge great big girl and this tiny wee ploughman. She used to sit
him on her knee, and look after him like a baby. She learnt a lot
because of this wee guy. She learnt more than I did.

I complained to the Land Army people. They knew what was happening. They were sending girls to domestic work

But they didn't expect you to complain about it – it was
wartime. I wanted to market garden. I said to them "Look, I'm
going to leave unless I get some market gardening." They said
"Alright, you can go to MacBraynes." This was a big fruit farm.
MacBrayne agreed to take me but he warned me that it would
by nothing but hoeing. And it was. I couldn't bear it and I had
to pack it in. I went to the Land Army office, and boy, did I
catch it! "I wasn't loyal – I signed a contract – I should keep my
word" blah, blah, blah. I said I didnae want to hoe and that was
the end of the matter. He said "Right, you're dishonourably
discharged." I went back to the same draughtsman's office.

In your contract with the Home Guard it said that you were
supposed to learn something about the land, but they never
taught you anything. You were cheap labour. Often my money
was short, but who could you complain to? I never even got my
uniform. I was dying to wear it. All I got was a pair of
dungarees and gumboots.

Where I lived there was far more resentment about Land Army girls than ever there were about evacuees

2nd West Country Girl Like the evacuees, they were accused of
bringing lice to the village. They were considered tarty. I've got
two brothers and I can hear my mother now. I was a lot
younger than my brothers. They were in their late teens. My
mother used to do my hair because it was very long and in plaits.
Whilst she plaited it she used to take her vengeance out on these
Land Army girls. "Bloody Land Army girls" – Tug, tug – "I
told ———— and ———— to keep away from them." Both
brothers got girls pregnant.

The Land Army girls were down at Steanbow, which is still a

farm now. It was a great motorbike age and after work they used to fly down there on their motorbikes and go to Wells pictures and all over the place. Whereas before they had a selection of village girls, which was very limited, they now had a vast harem of girls from as far away as Newcastle, which was a foreign land to them. Because at that time there wasn't the pill and what have you, you automatically married them.

Somerset Farmer The first Land Army girl we had, she was a lovely girl in every way but she was absolutely hopeless when it came to working on a farm. She came from London. She came down to Steanbow Training Farm because she was afraid she would have to go to Manchester and for some reason all these Land Army girls had a horror of going to Manchester.[3]

This girl's parents was not very practical because the girl didn't know the way to boil a kettle to make a cup of tea, or to boil an egg.

We were married, my husband and I, the beginning of 1940. We had a local boy, to start off with, but he decided to join up. He wanted to get married, and if he got married his wife got an allowance – a separation allowance, and she could save that until such times as he came out of the war. So then we had the Land Army girl. She was 18 or 19. She was hopeless. She couldn't do anything, so we notified Steanbow and they had her back and we had a second Land Army girl.

She came from Greenwich. She had the same tale – she joined the Land Army because she didn't want to go to Manchester. She was a good girl for farmwork. She took to it. She could do milking, though she didn't like a kicking cow. If my husband was busy mowing and I had to take his part in the cow stall any cow that was difficult to milk, or any cow like a heifer that hadn't been broken in, or you were breaking in, that was my lot to milk. But even so, she was a good girl. You could send her out with the horse. With the Land Army girls you had to pay them a regulation wage, and there was an amount fixed how much you could deduct for board and how much you had to pay for overtime.

---

[1] Britain was the first country to force women into the services and key wartime industries when the National Service (No. 2) Act became law, 18

[2] Royal Ordnance Factory.
[3] Metropolitan Vickers and A. V. Roe were engaged on aircraft production in the Manchester area. One reason for extending the age of conscripted women up to 51 was to release younger women for aircraft production, where there was a chronic shortage of workers.

12 Production was production

London Woman When Stan first went in the army they sent him to Nottingham. They used to march down this street and this woman asked Stan and a few others if they'd like to have a bath.

Her husband She was very,very good to us. Her husband was a miner. He took Marge and me down the mine. Never again. This was 1940. Before they were modernised. We had to sign to go down, that they wouldn't be held responsible if anything happened. We went right to the coalface. Went by train, in this little truck underneath. On a Sunday morning he took us. You were sitting humped up. It was bloody terrible. The miners were working flat on their bellies. I don't know whether they still do it. It was shocking. Hacking it out. We had to turn our lights off. It was a terrible feeling. Terrible. Deathly silence. All you could hear was the trickle of water.

Miner 1937 – work was changing. Everywhere. They was after production. They knew as this war was going to come off. In 1937 they was putting your wages up. From 7/7d you raised to ten bob; from 9/7d you raised to thirteen bob. If you was a collier, from 9/11d (I'm talking about day rate minimum) they went onto piecework. If you couldn't get your stint out, if you was in a place where it was hard, you was still guaranteed a basic wage of £1 per shift. That was £6 a week.

When the war was on they started Pit Production Committees. So many miners was on them, but they was union men

– full-time officials. They'd come down the pit and have a look around – inspecting, and this that and the other. Every pit had a board strung up. All the collieries from Wigan to Manchester area was on the board giving the production every day. If you'd drawn more than your tonnage off the pit they put a flag on top. That flew. You got so much extra money for that. Everybody got that except that little lad that was fetching the stuff to you. He didn't get a ha'penny. That was the haulage hand. I was working in a seven foot seam at Moston in what they call "Foxholes", and it was foxholes too. Inferior coal. It wasn't fit to burn on a boiler. They were taking anything out! Production was production. It was only dust! No matter where you went, they were opening districts out.

That was one of the reasons for the 1944 strike. They wanted a bit too much out of the miners and they wouldn't pay for it. The owners were trying to force you to work in districts that had been closed because of fire. I'll name you a few: The William Pit, The Haig – how many disasters were there? They were opening up districts where men had been killed and left in. They was trying to open them up again and get men to work in them. I went into one – the Lightbowne in Moston Colliery.

It was closed for over 20 years and they said "Go and open it up." They sent a dozen of us to take the brickstoppings out at the main level, to go in. When you go through the main doors you have to shut this door to open the middle one, and then shut that to open the other one, on account of air pressure. When you go in you can smell the must in the air. The stagnant air. Keep down – don't rise above your standing height or else: curtains. You was on the deck. When we went in there all we were sending out were coke, not coal. It was burnt to hell. And then when we got to the coal face it was red hot. Get out! We was working with nowt on and just us clogs. It was putting lamps out as quick as you were getting them lit. Get out of it! Cor.

Nobody liked it when the Bevin Boys came in. The Bevin Boys, some of them was glad they hadn't got to go in the army

The Bevin Boys were conscripts sent down the mines. You got

all sorts as Bevin Boys. Sons of land owners, besides mill lads,
what was the age of 18, 'cos they were drafted in.

We was asked to take so many Bevin Boys after they'd done
their training on the top. That was 90 days down the pit but you
couldn't take them near the coalface. They was only allowed on
fetching timber in from the airways. You see, you've got so
many different roads. You've got top, middle and main – that
was where your coal was coming from. Your middle was a
good retreat if anything happened. Your top was where all
timber went in – at the top of the face and was distributed all
down the face. What ever was wanted, from four foot props to
ten foot. They used the Bevin Boys for bringing timber or on
the roadways, or tramming – shoving the tubs from the main
places to where it was wanted. In some parts they did have what
they called a trainee face.

The gaffers came to you and said "I want you to take 3 or 4
Bevin Boys." You knowed they'd had their training on the top
and that they had to come down the pit, but you was under a
liability because if a lad got killed it was our fault because we
were supposed to be training them. Even if he only got a nick in
his little finger – we were liable. They wasn't allowed near the
face. If they were doing any mischief they was near on getting
themselves killed, on the coal belts and pans, and one thing and
another. They used to venture near the bottom of the face.
We'll say the fire man was on and he was firing shots – there
was a big responsibility there, 'cos I seen one Bevin Boy near on
run into danger. We'd said they were firing shots and he says
"Where? Where?" and he were going to run towards it. "Gert
out!" – we knocked him out of the road – "Get thi bottle and
get off! Get as far along the face as tha can." But you had to
work with them so there was no sense in resenting them. You
got to fetch them into the company.

Another thing during the war was the Tribunals, We'll say
you're absent Monday, work Tuesday, play Wednesday, work
Thursday, go for your wages Friday, and that was it – you were
first in pub. If you were a collier you went in front of a
Tribunal. They stopped you on the coalface. You wasn't
allowed near a coalface after that. Your money was dropped.
You was still working at the pit, but on haulage, on haulage

68 rate. They wouldn't let you back onto the face until they thought you'd learnt your lesson.

Electrician, Ex-Communist Party Member About six weeks after the war started I was asked by the union to go up to Liverpool, to the Docks, because they had a terrific problem with organisation. Foulkes[1] was the union bod up there. At this stage we were concerned with building up the union and protecting the Party, as we were Commie-Nazis as far as the bastards were concerned.[2] I made quite a success up there but I got my call-up papers and where I was working the Essential Works Order didn't apply, so the union advised me to go down to the London Docks where the EWO[3] was applying, and that way I wouldn't be called up. By this time Germany had attacked Russia and we were fully supporting the war. I found when I got down there that there was an awful lot of reactionary trade unionists in charge of the docks. Take the problem of dilution.

The young electricians didn't want the dames in the docks because they realised that if the dames came in they'd be in the forces or drafted elsewhere

We had a hell of a fight to get the girls established. I was given one of them because they knew my attitude to bringing the girls into the docks, and getting on with the war effort. She was one of the first dozen who were introduced for the first time in the Green and Siley Weir – "Green and Slimey" at Albert Dock. These girls were put through training schemes run by the Ministry of Labour. The girl I got, Jess, was 21. Course, most of the boys, when the girls were there, all they were thinking about was getting the girls down in the bunk and having a bit of crumpet!

I made a terrific impression on the rest of the workforce because I taught her how to handle her tools properly. In fact she got to handling her tools so well that she was handling them like a born mechanic. I had boilermakers and shipwrights queuing up like swallows on a line, just to watch her work.

Once we'd got the girls accepted they then introduced the

Obviously they didn't want to go. The whole of the electrical dock labour force in London was up in arms over this question. Some of their leaders – reactionary types – were really rubbing their hands. They were going to have me over a barrel. The masses were all behind them and they wanted to see how I came up and tackled this. I had a very difficult job at this particular meeting on the ship, because all the rotten bastards who were trying to dodge the column were with me on this one. They were well in with the firm. They wouldn't be drafted. It would be the militants and the other boys who would get it.

All these lumps of shit got up and spoke first about why the boys should go. The overwhelming majority were of course against it, and they got me on toast. They said "What about you ————? You've been preaching greater war production all the time – now let's see your working-class ideas." I had quite a raw bash. They accepted the point about if we lost to Hitler we'd have no trade unions at all but I didn't convince them on the issue of making the best use of manpower. I did later on, but not at that time.

When the war broke out, on the dock we were only casual labourers

Liverpool Docker You tried to get hired and if you didn't you went to Rimrose Road and you signed on in the Clearing House. With casualisation it was very easy for the bosses to blacklist people. They did it to me. I was ten years unemployed before the war. I wasn't alone. There was three thousand in my branch unemployed, and the union done nothing about that. And men, not registered dockers, were being employed because they weren't paying them the full rate. When the war broke out and we were still casual workers we had a card, not a tally, not a Board of Trade tally, but card which stated on it "His Majesty's Government. Required for Urgent Work". It was stamped with your number on it. You was hired of a morning, at a ship's stand. The card's taken off you. It's kept until five o'clock, when they gave it you back. You're only on for the day. The bosses wouldn't have it any other way. They were used to casual labour. It was hire and fire.

We started as permanent workers in 1940. When the Essential Works Order Bill went through the House, in it was the de-casualisation of dockers and the docks taken over by the government. That meant government money to the employers. They were well compensated because every one of them inflated their wage bill. No exceptions. One time-keeper I know, he wasn't a time-keeper at all! He was the same as myself – an ordinary docker, but he was picked up by a firm and made a timekeeper. He looked after the firm's interests. He got a fiddle for them and he got a fiddle for himself by inflating the wage bill, which he said was his instructions.

Know what the fiddle was? The more money they paid out in wages they had 10% on top of that from the government to cover their bill

With Liverpool being the major port for the North Atlantic trade all ships carrying explosives never entered the Mersey. They were diverted to Holyhead.[4] I worked at Holyhead at them. I was a foreman there. I took a gang of me own with me. Everybody's searched on the pier at Holyhead. You've got to take your boots off and you've got to put canvas shoes on, and your matches and cigarettes are all taken. When you've done your job you come back to the pier, get off the Police Patrol boat and your gear's taken out of the little lockers that it's in and given to you and you got paid your wages on the railway station. I'll tell you how good it was.

As a foreman I was paid two bob a day extra plus two bob a day explosives – four bob a day over and above the basic rate – which was £15 a week. When we went to Holyhead the train fare was paid for us. We used to get the Irish Mail to Holyhead. When the pay-day come up you get in the queue at the railway station – at the box where you get your tickets. The time-keeper's in there and he's got the list. You walk in and give your tally number and your name, to identify yourself, even though they know you. You tell the man what you want. You do that even in the clearing house – how much you want. You never ask exactly for what you want – you spring it by about five to six bob. You don't get it if it's not been booked for you, but there's always the chance they've made a mistake in the book, and then you have it. My father learnt me that.

Anyhow, I'm at the counter, before me brother. My brother's behind me, Frankie. He was an air raid warden. I thought to myself, about £18. I said "£18 ten." And he pays me £18 ten. I says to Frankie "Sing out good." So he sings out good, goes the same as me, and gets it! There was a fiddle on. They were inflating the wage bill and getting their 10% on top from the government. You was making it for them! But you was getting a bit of a cut out of it.

In 1943 I was Chairman of the Strike Committee. We had a complete stoppage – Birkenhead, New Ferry, Rock Ferry, Bromborough and all them were out

I had contact with every union branch and every responsible person in the union from those areas. One of the main issues was that we hadn't had a wage increase for over 20 years before the war, and we hadn't had one since the war started. We were working 12 hours a day, sometimes more. Often you'd be straight home, straight to bed and up the next morning. Never had time to take the missus out or see the kids. That's how bad it was.

The '43 strike started in the Coast Line. It was a tuppence-ha'penny timber ship. The job was being done by a firm which was not registered with the Dock Labour Board. In other words – a scab firm. And it was tending to pay scab wages. So the dockers working at the ship decided to knock off. The Dock Labour Board told men to go to that ship and work it, but when they discovered what had happened they walked away from it. And then I got involved.

I had a meeting on the Wall. I told the men there was a dispute in the Coast and they wanted to watch it didn't spread. "We're not involved at the moment, but we can be if we don't do something about it. I'm going up there to find out what the score is." When I get up there I meet them outside the gate. Big tall feller – Irish bloke – he said "Where are you from?" I said "A1." He said "Get back to A1. We don't want no help." "You can't manage it on your own, because I'm going to be sent to work there, where you're chucking it. And then I'll be in it, and if I'm in it I'm going to have some say about it. Don't worry about that."

The strike eventually spread to my area. I had another meeting on the Wall. "Well, it's here boys. Some of our men have been sent to this bloody ship and have come back. We're going on strike until we get a public inquiry; an increase in wages and shorter hours. Agreed?" "All agreed." "I believe they're having a meeting on the Railway side at the bottom of Church Street. We'll go down there."

We all marched along there, the whole lot of us and I went on the platform. Our Branch Secretary was speaking but the crowd doesn't like union officials. They do nothing about anything. So they were howling and shouting at him. I walked up and said "Excuse me Tommy, this doesn't concern you. It concerns me, with all due respect to you." I addressed the men. I told them that what we wanted was a general mass meeting covering the whole port, and that we go to the Transport and General Workers' Union with that. At the meeting we elected a 12 man delegation which was representative of the whole area. I was from No. 1, there was a feller from No. 2 and so on.

We went to Transport House where I got told the District Committee would be in session. They gave full support to the proposition of a general mass meeting. But where were we going to have it? Nobody had any ideas. I went from there, down the stairs into Mr Mann's office – the Area Secretary. A flunky wanted to put me off. I said "No, it's Mr Mann I've come to see. There are 12 representatives here." "What's it about?" "That's our business. It's Mr Mann's business as well. It'll concern him." Eventually we were shown in.

Mann was sitting behind a big desk. "Sit down boys, sit down. What is it Joe?" "We're on strike. As is inevitable. You all sit on your bottoms and wait until it hits the whole port. Well, it's done it. We were the last. You've watched it all week spreading and developing." "Not our fault" he said, "It's the Dock Labour Board." "You can't blame the Dock Labour

Board if you agree to it. You've got to look into this," – and I gave him the proposals.

All strikes during the war were unofficial. We got threatened with bloody troops, police and everything

"My God" he said, "You're asking for something, aren't yer?" "Yes" I said "but we're the T & G don't forget – strongest union in the country, and our section is the lifeblood of that union. As the Dockers' Union we started the T & G, and we play the key role in it. I want a mass meeting and a public inquiry." "What do you mean by a public inquiry?" "Exactly what I say. We nominate a man representing us, and if they don't accept him I'll be prepared to accept one nominated by them, providing it suits the men." "Fair enough" he says "I just want to get these things right before I get in touch with London, with Jack Donovan.[5] But where are we going to have this mass meeting? That's one for me!"

I walked out and rang the White City Stadium in Breck Road, Liverpool. The owner is a friend of mine. It's a dog track. It's got a beautiful foyer and bar and all the facilities. I said "I'm speaking on behalf of the Transport and General Workers Union. We're out on strike and I'm of the opinion that to get the men solidly united, whether to go back to work, or to stop out – and we've been threatened with troops and God knows what – to get it clarified we want a mass meeting in your White City Stadium." "When would you want it for?" "It'd have to be sometime in the morning." "How about 11 o'clock?" "That'll do me" I said. "Good luck Byrne" he said, "You can have it, but don't mention my name to them". "I won't, but you ring Mr Mann and tell him you've got your loudspeakers already rigged – that saves him the worry about that. You needn't tell him who you are. I'll have informed him by then that it's the White City Stadium because he'll have to get the leaflets out." I went back into the room and I said "It's the White City Stadium, Mr Mann. Will you get the leaflets out and the notice in the press? For 11 o'clock in the morning."

Well, I was there and so was our committee. We had a committee meeting in the foyer – how to carry on when we were on the platform. Whilst we were discussing it we were watching them coming in. Oh, the bloody place was packed! Bloody thousands there. The platform was rigged in the centre like a boxing ring, and there was nobody, at that stage, on the platform at the mike. I said "Someone's got to go on that platform with these proposals, because that's the basis of the whole meeting – whether they accept them or not. If they don't, the strike's still on. If they do accept them the strike's finished. Now you all understand that?" "Agreed." I said "I'm walking out there now." I left them and walked out.

I walked up to the little steps going up to the platform. You could have heard a bloody pin drop. Jack Donovan's standing there, right by the mike to do his little bit

Mann's sitting there. Jack Donovan looked round "What do you want?" "I'm going to use that." "You're not saying nothing here until I've said it. This is my meeting." "No it is not your meeting. It happens to be my meeting. I organised this. Not you. Is that right Mr Mann?" "It is Joe," and he says to Jack Donovan "You'd better let him speak first, because if he doesn't speak you're going to have no meeting. They'll all get up and go away and we won't be anywhere. The baby will be left with us. He's got the solution to the problem so let him deal with it." Jack said "I'm not agreeing, but I'll give way," and he gets out the road. I took about ten minutes.

I told them the strike should never have taken place in the first place, but now that it has, and we're all involved, it's got to be ended as soon as possible. "The country's in a state of emergency. We're threatened with troops by the Powers That Be. I'm not afraid of them, if you're not, but it's a risk we can't afford to take. That's why I'm here. There's the proposals. I'm putting them to you. If you accept them the next bit will be for Jack Donovan to get up here and for him to say that he accepts them on behalf of the National Docks Group, and the strike's over." "Hear! Hear!" "That's it Joe!" "Hear! Hear!" And Donovan's choked! He didn't get five minutes. They bloody howled him down.

I was the world's worst, as far as the press was concerned.

After the strike was over I took a hefty delegation up to the *Liverpool Record* with a factual statement, and seen the night editor. Do you know what he said to me? "You don't own the *Record*." I said "Neither do you. There's the truth," I said. "You publish that instead of publishing bloody rubbish – 'cos that's all the dockers think about it."

Somerset Farmer When my husband and I got married and got the farm we had between 50 and 60 acres. We had to have ploughed ground because the Agricultural Committee came round and told us. We had four fields out of our little bit ploughed up. It was the first time we'd done any arable, and yet there was someone only two farms away, if you go how the bird do fly, who had 100 acres and he never ploughed an inch. He reckoned none of his farm was suitable, and they never made him plough it. What he done, when the Ministry men came he deliberately took them where he knew stones was near the surface. He could get extra rations for his cattle – extra coupons for cake – extra potatoes, all manner of things we couldn't get, because he had no arable.

You had to pay for having your land ploughed. We had no equipment for ploughing. We hired the disc harrows. The County Agricultural Committee had contractors that you could contact and they would send a man with a tractor and plough, and plough your ground. When it came to sowing you had to go behind the tractor to work the drill. My husband nearly got poisoned doing that. He had to watch and make sure every one of these drills was letting seed out, that none of them did get blocked up with the soil. The tractor fumes did come back and come up round him and he was ill for two days with carbon monoxide poisoning.

Another time when they came he was really ill. He was under the doctor, he was so ill. I didn't know whether I was going to be a widow or not. It was the last field we had to plough up and two farmers came who were working for the Agricultural Committee and one of them turned round and said to me "If your bloody husband isn't fit to do the farming, let the bugger get out and let someone come in that will do it." I said, under my breath "You bugger! You ought to bloody drop dead" – and he were dead in six weeks! One of these farmers came from

Ditcheat and the other from Cranmore. They had big farms. They had plenty of men to do the work. They didn't know what it was to do a day's work.

When we had to plough up $4\frac{1}{2}$ acres of field for arable, we had to put wheat in. A man from the Ministry was supposed to come and examine the field in the spring to see that the field had been ploughed up and the corn planted. You didn't get your subsidy until about the time it was harvested. Come July or August time we had a cheque come for $4\frac{1}{2}$ acres subsidy on $4\frac{1}{2}$ acres of wheat. My husband sent it back.

They scratched their heads. "Farmer sent back a cheque for $4\frac{1}{2}$ acres of wheat subsidy for $4\frac{1}{2}$ acres of wheat?" They couldn't make it out. They sent a man to see us. "Why did you send the cheque back?"

What happened was that it was supposed to have been spring sown. We had to hire someone to come and cultivate it but it had been a very wet spring, and the contractor had got bogged down on the ground and by the time they got round to our farm it was too late to plough to put it down into corn. So he sowed some quick growing ley. Not wheat. "Do you know" this chap said "one of our Ministry men have been and examined your fields and he said that the wheat was growing well and that you had a good crop. We'll have to investigate this."

'Course, all the farms that this particular man had supposed to have inspected – they went round and hardly any of them had planted the wheat because of the wet weather. I think we were about the only one that had sent the subsidy back. The other farmers had to send their cheques back. The chap who had originally inspected got the sack.

Her Husband Some of these inspectors, they'd come round in their cars and some of the farmers would give them a glass of cider and they would go off without even bothering to look at the wheat. There was one man, if he were inspecting you, he'd come round and he'd say "You'd better plough up this ground" and if you said "I don't want to plough this ground up" he'd say "It's alright – we'll sign the paper and say it is ploughed." The farmer got so much for it and the Ministry man got so much.

Somerset Farmer We were working from 6 in the morning to 12 at night. We had double summertime and we'd stay out in the hayfield until it was getting dark. We had an elevator and a tractor and we used to hire other men to come and help us with the haymaking. They'd go home and then the cows would come in, and many a night my husband and I started milking between 11 o' clock and 12 o' clock. We'd be milking by hand because we didn't have a milking machine at that time and it'd be 2 o'clock by the time we'd finished milking our cows and washed down the cow stall and scrubbed out the dairy – and we had to be up again next morning. We had 32 cows and 12 head of young stock. My husband got so tired the doctor put him on they benzedrine pills, to keep him awake.

Factory Worker I was living with my parents in Dagenham and I went to work for Briggs. I started down the River Plant on night work. They had a contract for petrol cans, what they used in the desert – the big square ones. They was also doing cans for other firms, like Jowetts. They didn't do Fords until Fords bought them out. I soon got used to factory work. There was no problem, even with night work. The petrol can contract run out and we all got took on up the Main Plant. I got put in the wood mill. You've got to remember a lot of cars and vans then had wood in them – wooden beams that went across lorries, and the flooring and the sides. This was day work. A week's wages then, and I was doing round about 56 hours, was, for someone my age, three pound thirteen. Coming from Wapping where I'd been getting thirty bob I thought I was a millionaire. I was getting more than my old man. He was a cook and he was picking up three pound ten.

I would say at Briggs the paramount element was not war production, it was how much you were going to pick up at the end of the week. It was the money

In them days, how filthy you got at work was how you went home. You worked right up to the minute. You was glad to clock out and get away from the place. I can remember going home and my mother saying "Aye, aye – here comes the worker" 'cos I was in a hell of a state. At Briggs you didn't have canteens like we've got today. We used to have tea barrows came round – we still have – but they was more predominant then. There was no hot grub. It was cakes and rolls. Anything hot you brought in yourself, like a flask of soup.

Because of war production we was working hell of long hours. The time for knocking off was 5 o'clock. What they used to do – all of a sudden about 4 o'clock they'd put a blackboard and easel (just like in a schoolroom) at the bottom of the woodmill, and they'd say "Knocking off time 6 o'clock." Just like that. If you wanted to go you had to give a reason! Then, round about half past five they'd come out and scrub the "6 o'clock", "7 o'clock." They'd then give you the facility to go round the cafe and have a cup of tea and a bun. All this would be because they were behind with some order.

When the siren used to go we used to clock in of a morning at 8 o' clock and straight out to the shelter. We used to clock off to go home for dinner, come back, clock in, on your way back and straight back to the shelter. Five o' clock: clock out and go home! This went on for weeks. 'Course, the company got their heads together. "We can't have this. We're getting no production."

We were out in the shelters playing pitch and toss, or cards, or watching the old dogfights overhead. It was lovely! But then they stopped that, didn't they?

They came up with the idea where they had light bulbs all around the plant, painted red, and they had spotters on the roofs. As soon as them spotters got a warning of an imminent attack these light bulbs used to go on and off. So there you were, working with one eye on your job and one eye on the light bulbs, waiting for it to go so you could shoot out. Soon as that light went on you shut your machine off and you was away.

We used to have women working in the woodmill then. Everything being done in wood meant half of it was un-seasoned. It came from Malaya, Singapore, South America – all over the place. It used to stink terrible when you were cutting it. The spray used to come off it. It was then taken out the back to be dipped in green paint to preserve it. One day there was a couple of women pushing a barrow load of timber out into the dip to be dipped and lights started going on and off, and the general foreman – he's out the office, down the stairs, and as the girls are about to go through the door, they're leaning, bent forward, pushing the barrow, and he's put one foot on their back and he jumps over the top of 'em and flattens 'em, and he's out the door. And he's the foreman!

They had a colossal number of women working down at Briggs. There was one department where they was doing steel helmets. They was all women. In the press shop they still had women working up until about 1950. They was working on the small presses. There was no resentment of the women working at Briggs. After the war – yes.

Conscientious Objector Through the anarchists I got to know a chap who had a contract from some War Department because he had an idea for a machine for curing frostbite. He had had some work before the war in some government medical research department. He was a brilliant feller. He persuaded them that he had a really brilliant idea for producing this frostbite machine.

Frostbite had knocked out a hell of a lot of soldiers in the Norwegian campaign and this was something, rather late, the British realised they'd given no thought to. He was funded in some modest way to set up a little workshop. In order to get equipment, which was very very short, he had an arrangement with the airforce for sending him scrap from factories and crashed planes to his little workshop.

He got round him a team of about six to ten (it varied a bit) conscientious objectors, one or two people who had been excused military service, a couple of chaps who were on the run and at least one deserter from the army. We were working in this little place. Every month a lorry would come, loaded with all these sacks of scrap and they'd all get turned out into the basement. Upstairs we had what was the beginnings of the laboratory – which was never built and never finished! But what we did have was a whole little series of tables and a little manufacturing process was going on.

Part of the scrap we got were copper coils covered with silver – some mysterious bloody thing – and they were about $2\frac{1}{2}$–3 inch diameter. They were just right for ladies bracelets! We were snipping these things off in two or three curls, slightly bending the end in and polishing them all up (they came covered in grease, crap and dirt). We got some other tiny spring things which we dipped in enamel and stuck on the end and there we were: tatty little Utility type bracelets, which were absolutely impossible to get!

One of the guys who was a smooth talker used to go off all round the country getting orders, selling to Bentalls of Kingston, John Lewis stores, Selfridges – all over the country. The stores were falling over themselves to buy these little things. We couldn't make enough of them! There was a whole team of us making a living out of this scrap. No questions were asked, as it was coming from official sources. After all, he was working on this frostbite machine! The heat was off, as far as it was concerned. The fighting was going on in the desert rather than Norway.

It was at this time that I was asked – the only time in the war – for my identity card. We were sitting in a cafe in Camden Town when the police came in and checked everyone's identity. A policeman asked for my identity card and asked me what I did for a living. I said "I'm afraid I can't divulge that. Government job." "Oh" he says "very good sir."

When Anita and her sister lived in a hostel in 1944 and the manageress got up and said "All the virgins in this hostel I can get in a telephone booth", I instantly thought of my two cousins

Anita And I've regretted it ever since!
London Boy The hostel was run by a government department. It was specially built for industrial workers. We came from all over Britain.
Anita We had a good time, didn't we?
London Boy I had a marvellous time. This was in Coventry.
Anita We were all there.
London Boy Your brother went first. I volunteered. I was only 15. The only way I could earn money was to go there. Plenty of work in London, but fifteen bob a week. When I went there my money went up to £5 a week. By 17 I was earning £10. Mind,

you paid a lot of tax. It was the money. I went there because of that, I'll be honest. Our factory was the most modern in Europe. It was built in 1940. It was Standard. It was what they called a Shadow factory. They made aero engines there and Standard run it. Compared with what I'd worked in London it was smashing. In fact the factory then, in 1941, the machinery was better there than what I'm working with now. That's no exaggeration. And the conditions were better than what I'm working under now.

Anita I had a cushy job. I was an inspector. I always had to wait until the section had completed their work before I could inspect it, so I used to go off and see my sister in the machine room. We used to have a talk and a little flirt with the boys. I had a rip-roaring time. Life at home was restricting. There was a lot of domestic responsibilities because we had a big family. It was our freedom, as youngsters, to get away from home.

London Boy It was like a big holiday camp, except you had to work. Coming from homes with no baths and hot water it was a luxury for many. You were living in dormitories. At the end of each dormitory of each block you had a little writing room, and then there was the main block where you had dances and the canteen and where they showed pictures.

Anita The community living was very nice and you didn't have any domestic responsibilities. And the boys! There were hundreds of boys! It was lovely.

London Boy In the hostel there were about 600 women and 400 blokes. There had been about 61 women had to leave because they had been made pregnant, and it had only been open a year and a half.

---

[1] Frank Foulkes, who after the war was expelled from the ETU, with others, for having interfered with postal ballot returns to secure the election of a Communist General Secretary.

[2] Due to the Nazi-Soviet Non-Aggression Pact of 23 August 1939.

[3] Essential Works Order.

[4] This presumably happened after the Liverpool May Blitz. During the blitz the steamer *Malakand* was berthed in Husskisson Dock, Liverpool, and its cargo of 1,000 tons of high explosive bombs blew up.

[5] Jack Donovan, National Secretary of the Docks Group of the TGWU.

13 The King says to me "How do you like the army?" I told him I didnae like it

Fusilier Before the invasion of Normandy, the King – King George – came to inspect us. My usual experience was that I ended up being the person who was spoken to. This occasion wasnae any different. The King says to me "How do you like the army?" I told him I didnae like it. He said something like "Private something or another, there are lots of things you've got to do during the war." If looks could have killed me, everybody that passed me committed murder.

Scunthorpe Man I didn't take to army life at first. From Scunthorpe we went to Newcastle and then we were posted to the Orkneys. We were there because of Scapa Flow. We were a searchlight battery. We were in nissen huts on Orkney. They had to have them strapped down because of the wind. I was 18 months on Orkney. Too long. We got off once. I think it was a fortnight. We had no social life. I have heard since that Gracie Fields and one or two big stars went to Orkney to entertain, but we never saw them! At one time we all used to play cowboys and Indians! There was just nothing to do. It was so bad, some of them shot themselves. A sergeant shot himself.

Whilst we were there some paratroopers came up one time because they wanted volunteers for Airborne. Some of us went and some of us didn't. I think they did this on purpose. They knew the morale of the troops would be low, and that's how they used to pick them up.

Paratrooper I went into the forces the early part of 1942. I was in the RAF at first but I got transferred to the army. Prior to D day they were building up the army. They took all the A1 blokes out of the airforce and navy and transferred them to the army. For a minute, a minute before 12 we were civvies. We could have hopped it and they couldn't have done anything. But we were stuck out in the wilds of Lancashire, so it wouldn't have done us any good, and the camp was well guarded.

When I joined the army we were shoved over to Ireland, Northern Ireland, at the foot of the Mountains of Mourne. It was a hell of a bloody place. Drizzling with rain every day. One day they sat us all in the canteen and we were thinking "What the bleeding hell's going on here?" Next thing we knew there was a warrant officer and a sergeant come on the stage. They were in the Parachute Regiment. They showed us a parachute, how it worked, opening it out. I said to me mates "'Ere, if we join that mob we'll get away from this bleeding place." We all goes up and volunteers. We have our medicals and it turns out that out of the 12 of us that came out the RAF I'm the only one that's passed his medical. I was lumbered! I was going to leave all my mates. Not only that – it turns out that I've still got to stay in Ireland for 3 months! I had to do another lot of groundwork.

I jumped 32 times. I was on experimental jumping as well. They had half the parachute missing. It was great. You only got nerves the second time you jumped. The first time you didn't know, but the second time you knew and you was like jelly. It was out of a balloon. You've got to make the effort to get out. With an aircraft the slipstream got you, and you was away. You never had no chance to change your mind. But in a balloon you're 800 foot up, and when you look down . . . One of my mates on the ground who was waiting his turn, when he saw me afterwards he said "Every one of you, every time you came out you were screaming your bleeding heads off." I said "You was the same."

Detention Centre Inmate The vast majority of cases in detention, when I was in, were what they called "non-reporters". These were youngsters who, nine cases out of ten, were illiterates – people who couldn't either read or write – they couldn't read their notices for call-up. They were really backward, nervous young people. When they were caught they had to do a short period – three months or less, I believe, before they entered the service. The others would be people who were absent without leave, of longer than a certain period, otherwise it could be dealt with by confinement to barracks. They were a large proportion. Then we had a strange category of people who had trained as paratroopers, but when it came to it, wouldn't jump. They were given 84 days as a standing thing, if they continued to refuse to jump after their training period.

84 Oxford Lad The first three or four years in the army were very, very bad, because I thought the war was never going to end at all. If you ever made a complaint about anything, like the food, you got punished. They'd take your name and the next thing you know, you're on fatigues in the cookhouse. They got you doing all sorts of stupid things like whitewashing the stones around the nissen hut with a little toothbrush, or they had us blacking the bottoms of our boots. It was all spit and polish. We had a mirror in the middle of the nissen hut. You had to look in that before you went out, because the guards on the gate were watching to see if you were properly dressed. There'd be a few MPs in the town and they'd try and catch you out, for having hands in your pockets and that sort of thing. And you always had to dodge the MPs on the railway stations.

Once we had a Warrant Officer, P.T. bloke, very strict. I had a travel warrant to travel home. You had to leave fairly early and I got a chit so that I could, because the connection was at Bletchley. I was walking down (and in the Services you obey the last order) and this Warrant Officer saw me. "Where are you going?" I said "I'm going out." "You were," he said "Get back." And I had to change back into denims again and had to go down the lecture room. They were talking about Mills bombs – how to strip them. I couldn't go that night. I had to go the next morning. For punishments they would have you running around the square with full kit on, holding your rifle above your head. I had to do that many times. Or if your kit wasn't laid out properly they used to come round and knock it all over the floor and you'd get detention. But I sort of got used to army life after those first years. In fact I signed on again in 1945 because I'd got so used to the services by then and I was worried about coming back to unemployment in civilian life.

London Tailor Army life was a kind of life I had not previously experienced before, except during periods of unemployment. It was a life of no effort, except for short spurts, like an hour on the barrack square, but the rest of the time was a great big scrounge. What I revolted against was that I was so bored and I was constantly upset by the pettiness of the authority. I learnt all the scrounges possible – you never walked without a piece of paper or a pail in your hand because if you're going nowhere, they'll find you somewhere to go. You can't be walking nowhere in a barracks, that's for sure. "You! Where are you going?" And if you're not going anywhere they find you some fatigue.

In all the units I was in, because they were not fighting units the discipline was quite relaxed, so there was not too much discontent. Except for one incident. We were guarding an aerodrome in the Midlands, between Leicester and Derby. We were a detachment of about 40 or 50 men. The majority of us were doing 24 hour guards, on and off. It was a transport command. One of the officers, a middle-aged bloke, was a hardcase. He felt very important and he was a bit regimental, which was not on. On a detachment it never is. That's OK in a barracks where the Colonels are about and the Majors are about, but you don't expect a Lieutenant to be regimental out on a small detachment.

This bugger used to creep around at night, in his plimsolls, trying to catch blokes having a smoke or a kip. It was getting a bit much, him creeping around. He was bound to catch you! There wasn't a duty that you didn't snatch a smoke or try and have your head down for ten minutes. Out in the middle of nowhere we didn't expect all this shit. It was such a loosely run unit, we used to collect 4d a man for the cook to buy little extras, like spices and things. The cook had previously been a ships cook and we were having a life of O'Riley, except for this sod who kept us on our toes on guard – which was the worst thing about being there, because on the 24 hours off it was a doddle. We would go into town or go and have a drink. Everybody was seething about this sod.

One night somebody let a round off, across his bows. That put a stop to it. The bloke who did it said he thought he saw somebody looking very suspicious and when he couldn't get a reply to his challenge he put a round over his head, to stop him. The officer never again crept around in his plimsolls. On the contrary! He'd be half a mile away and he'd be shouting "It's alright sentry, Orderly Officer here, sentry."

ATS Woman I didn't like the fatigues in the army. I didn't like being told what to do and being told to be up by seven and to be in by a certain time. If you went out on your half day off you still had to be in by a certain time. There was no freedom. It was worse than being at school.

The first battery I was posted to was in Kenilworth near Coventry. This was after the Coventry Blitz. We were two miles up a remote country lane. We were in Nissen huts with latrines. When it rained it used to come in and pour on your bed. The Medical Officer came round and he simply told us to move our beds in between the drips.

I was on a height-finder, which was a machine to find the actual height of a plane. You could only use that during daylight, and you didn't get much action during the day. It was mostly at night, and then you went down and I was a height computer. You had to get the bearing and angle. I was terrified of the guns going off. At one battery we had 4.8's but mostly it was 3.7's. We were taken out of the Royal Artillery in 1944 because we weren't wanted any more – because of D day, and we were transferred to the Royal Army Ordnance Corps.

I was married in 1944, and then I discovered I was pregnant. I got an automatic discharge in the February of 1945. When I was first stationed at Kenilworth quite a lot of girls were having babies. There was one girl – I was going on leave – and she walked with me, and she was very nice and very very young. Because of that we had to have medicals every month. We used to line up, stripped to the waist. It was sometimes said that girls wanted babies to get out of the services, as if you were pregnant it meant an automatic discharge. We had quite a rash of them.

I was shanghaied into bloody army. I didn't want to go but I had no alternative

Boy Soldier It was proposed by bloody headmaster at school. I was living with my grandmother, and that was hell. Family were split up. Even as boy soldiers we were on regular routine. We were on peacetime establishment but first and foremost you were a soldier. The discipline was absolutely fucking . . . Well, you wouldn't credit it. When it came to educating boy soldiers it was just bloody sadistic. Absolutely sadistic. When you were doing drill they used to put a brush down your arms, behind your back, put their knee in your back, and you've got

this stick over your elbows. This was regular. We were trained   **87**
in Signals, but everyone, no matter what their trade, had to
learn to shoot a rifle. We used to go up to range and fire so
many shots each week. I was shooting 303's at 14.

Driver, North African Campaign I still believe the finest
general of the second world war was Rommel. A soldier and a
gentleman. When he over-run Tobruk, and over-run a hospital
he personally went round and see if there was anything he
could do for the wounded – British and allied wounded.
Montgomery was a . . . He brought his Leyland Retriever,
which was made into a mobile living quarters, he brought it in
for a job to be done on it. Bleeding thing – where it could be
locked up, it was locked up. He had a 24 hour guard on the
bleeding thing. They couldn't lock the cab up because you've
got to work on it. He used to sit in it and read a passage from
the Bible or a prayer book, then he'd work out what sort of
push he'd have tomorrow. When he drove into Tripoli he
automatically closed all the brothels. That made him very
popular!

**Old Churchill came over at Alamein, just prior to the push, and
come up with his cigar and his V – Victory sign. "Better times
around the corner." And we were going "And when are you going
to get us home, you pot-bellied old bastard?"**

When it was June you'd not work from twelve to five. Siesta. it
was daylight till ten, half past, so you'd make up that leeway
and work from 5 to 10. Tanks were coming back needing
repairs, lorries were coming back, needing repairs. You had to
get cracking on it because there was a push on. You were far
enough back to work in comparative safety, although no-one's
safe when there's a bomber about. We were cutting up rough at
Suez because we were working during the day and then, as soon
as we were finished, they got us digging trenches – slit trenches.
We weren't happy about that.

There was a lot of muttering going on. We used to be able to
get into Suez and go to the pictures. Now that we were digging
these bloody slit trenches all that suddenly stopped. We dug
them because they said if they didn't hold him at El Alamein

we'd be so thin on the ground after that, he'd push straight through Alex, straight past the Pyramids, through Cairo and straight down. As it happens, of course, they held him at Alamein knowing that they couldn't be encircled.

As a result of our mutterings the CO got us on parade. Captain Phillip Brownlow – "Pigshead". "It's been brought to my attention" he said "that there is mutterings. Men don't like what's happening. I don't know if you realise it, but up in the other side of Alex men are dying. The fact that you have been instructed to dig slit trenches means that if they're not held, you will have to stand in these trenches and defend your camp." Thanks a lot! He said "All I want to impress upon you people is that if this sort of muttering goes on, it's tantamount to mutiny – the punishment of which is death!" Nice fellow, we thought.

Company Sergeant Major, East Africa Berbera was the worst place I went to. That was one of the death cells of Africa. We should have been there three months. That was the limit, but we was there for nine months. It's a wonderful place to look at. It's on the Gulf of Aden. You're going down to the sea for about a day – you don't realise it but you're gradually going down and down, and it's getting hotter and hotter and hotter. When we were there about six months when we should only have been there for three they sent us up to a place called Sheikh. It was a bloody mountain in the middle of the desert. It took us 6 hours from the beach to get there. The road up it was one way. In the morning it was for going up, and the afternoon you were allowed to come down. When you got up, there was all greenery. There was goats and trees and everything. And there were all these bloody South Africans, all covered in sores and swollen lips and talking absolutely bloody silly. They had been there a year, and that's how they were. When we got there, there was me and my old mate George. We was thinking twice whether to go back. We was going to overdo our stay, but as we were NCOs . . .

When I got to Africa I was promoted and I was earning more than a Captain was in this country. Being a little higher station in life I was offered to be trained as an officer but I refused that as I knew I hadn't got the brains for that. I had a personal servant out there. The bulk of the senior army staff were whites, and then you had the artisans who were Asians, and then you had the wogs. I know a lot of people stick up for these blacks in this country, but as far as I was concerned they were savages in 1940.

When we got to India for some reason or other most of the guys seemed to take a completely different stance, as if they'd been set free in some kind of way. They became as bad as what I thought the Nazis was

Fusilier When we arrived in Kalyan the overall commanding officer took the whole shipload of us and said "Well you are now in India. Forget about your democratic ideas. This is a completely different situation here, and I'll expect you to treat these people – it was: these wogs – in the same way as the regulars have been treating them for hundreds of years." It was like giving everybody an individual licence to do what they effing well liked. And to be quite frank, they did.

The same day as we got this lecture from the Commanding Officer at Kalyan a couple of children came into the barracks. We're all lying in our charpoys, all out. Heat killing us. The children came round begging – and I would say there were about 20 to 30 blokes in the room, each side, and it's safe to say the majority of them were sitting with their penises out, waving them at the kids. "Come over here. Suck this." Some of them hit the kids, but these kids were so pushed around all through their life that they just took it. They didnae bother with it. I would suggest I was more affected than they were. I was over-sensitive to the situation. The kids came to me and I gave them some money and I finally got them out.

Then I got up on my bed and said "Listen, the lot of yous – there's no need for what you've done. If they're begging, we're partly responsible for their begging. If you don't want to give them just say "No, chase it" but all these actions that yous are making, exposing your penises and asking them to suck it, there's never any need for that. You're just degrading yourself, and putting yourself in the same situation as the people we're supposed to be fighting against – the Nazis." I'd have been as well talking to a brick wall.

Many of the guys there would have been just as comfortable sitting in a Nazi or SS uniform. It got to the stage where it looked as if I was going to have to fight everybody. I was there for a couple of weeks and by the time that we left not one individual would have said or touched one of the Indians while I was around. That's the kind of character I was. I was well known. I wasnae liked by the officers. They preferred the men to be the other way.

One of the big complaints about soldiers in the Far East – they called them the Forgotten Army – was that they werenae getting their mail. I know why they werenae getting their mail. The guys were half-inching it

In the first days I was in India I was sent to the Post Office department in Kalyan, where the mail was distributed through India to the front line. One of the cries in the Post Office department was "Wonder what's in that? Open it up!" If it was cigarettes or something they thought might be perishable they used to say "Och, he'll probably be dead." That's the reason why guys werenae getting their mail sometimes. It was nae a matter of going into the Post Office and regimental freedom-loving British soldiers saying "Oh yes, that's got to go to this regiment, they're up there fighting at the front." It was "What's in it! Let's see. Fags! Gie us that! Och, he'll be dead." That was the attitude. I daresay the guys at the front would have done the same if they'd been at the other end.

When I went out there they were only reforming the Chindits again. Wingate got killed in a crash, so they started up this second unit. If I remember right the first unit was made up of units like the Black Watch that had come from Tobruk, where they'd been slaughtered, and there were very few of them left. I believe the unit was even made up of deserters from the French Foreign Legion. Och, it was shambles their lot. When I went into it that was the situation – it was the tatters and remains. They were building it up into a fighting unit again.

I was in the Royal Scots Fusiliers at the time and suddenly, like that, I'm switched over and I was in the Black Watch, which was an airborne unit. Perhaps it was a good way of getting rid of a difficult character. Anyway, that's where I went, and I must confess the first night I spent there I lay all night in tears. And I was a tough character. Oh, it was terrible. It was like being planted in hell. I had salt burns right down each side of my face – just seeing the state of the men. Just bones. Just sitting – drinking jungle juice. My first impression was that I was in hell, and this was all the devils – thin arms, fighting one another. It was a madhouse. They were training us for a mainland landing. All the training was happening a hell of a quick. It was hell. We lost people in river crossings that were equal to anything you seen in that *North West Passage*. Often when I've seen that I've thought "Christ, that's like a bloody mill pond, compared to some of the stuff we used to negotiate." You don't need a human enemy to defeat you in the jungle.

I've been in marches – and this is no talking about being in action – this was patrols and training that lasted for 14, 15 days, where we were hacking our way through jungle with machetes. Officers with maps trying to figure out where there might be a water hole, and coming to a big salt lake and guys collapsing – men lying out, leaving them to die – I'm talking about dying with nothing happening. There was nothing you could do, except leave them. Nothing to do with Japanese.

As far as patrols in the jungles – most of the guys on both sides spent their time trying to avoid each other, if they could

You got the fanatical officer or the guy who wants a battle, but they were few and far between. First time I ever saw a Japanese was a prisoner of war. I shit myself, to be quite honest. You had heard all these tales, about all these horrible Japanese and how they fight to the death. On this occasion two Japanese were under the custody of an American guard. He asked us to give them our rifles, with our scabbard – bayonets – on them. It might sound pretty strange, but we just couldn't see that this was right to do, but eventually we gave our rifles, and the Japanese took up a stance to give us a demonstration in how they fought each other using bayonets. The American guy said "They're just like anybody else. For a few scraps of extra grub they'll show you anything. Even sell their granny." That was a big lesson. You were beginning to feel there wasn't much difference really, in a lot of ways, between how we felt and how they felt.

I could sit down and write page after page of atrocities that happened

I've a mate. A great bloke, honestly. He was a conscientious objector and lay in ———— Prison for nearly six months with no clothes, rather than put on the army uniform. That's what they done. Left them without any clothes. He eventually put it on. Once he put it on he gave up and become a soldier. He was in Imphal, and he had just come back out of the first Chindit trip. A great bloke, but in some ways evil with it. I seen him getting Indian women and raping them. Smashing their face in and raping until it got so bad that I had to fire at them to get them off. I was known. I had a reputation, and once I started threatening them, they got frightened. I seen things like that. Old women with their tits hanging down like chapatis – raping them. They'd women with kids, forcing them to squirt the milk out of their breasts. Things that were – if you seen it you'd say "Oh, that's Nazis," but that was British troops. Guys that you think butter wouldnae melt in their mouths in Britain. I'll never forget that. Never, never forget that. Never.

14 Don't you believe our navy had the edge on the German navy. Don't you believe it.

Chief Petty Officer I was on most boats, including submarines, but oh jeez – I hated submarines. Oh, when that bloody hatch was closed – Christ. It's deadly on a submarine. Bloody deadly it is. Though you don't pay much attention to it, you've always this fear in your belly. When war broke out, was I bloody glad I got transferred! I didn't ask to get transferred, but was I glad. I got down and kissed terra firma, when I got out. I think everybody was the same. In those days you didn't have a cat in hell's chance of getting up. That was it. It was curtains. They were so obsolete. Christ, everything you touched fell to bloody pieces, for lack of maintenance. Everything had been let slide. They hadn't kept up with the modern idiom as regards anything – guns, weaponry – anything. I'm not going to blame the Conservatives, even though they were in power at the time. It would be wrong to blame any government. It was the thing of the age – they thought the 1914–18 war was the war to end wars, like the last one was.

The navy was extremely strict on discipline. I think more strict than the other forces

But not with the brutality that you got in the army, although certainly brutality came into it on a lot of different ships. Don't forget, there's no backdoors in the navy. You can't run into the next field. This is the difference between the navy and all the other forces. You had to work together, your lives depended on it, so you had to be strict.

Normally the discipline was left to the PO, and you could get some wicked PO's. But in a way I suppose – and I came more or less right up from the bottom – although I was subjected to all this treatment, I think it did you a lot of good in some respects. I think in some cases, when the war broke out, the old-timers had got that bloody fed-up at getting new recruits who didn't know the first thing about seamanship, that they had to be bullies to make sure that you learned the right way. But some PO's I've seen knock AB's down gangways with their fists.

One of the worst, one of the notorious jankers jobs was you got put on painting. Oh bloody hell! You had to go round with a chipping hammer. That and in the galley – mountains of rotten greasy stinking pans. They were the worst. You had to be a very, very bad lad if you got the brig, and if you got the brig for more than 48 hours you've done something exceedingly bad, and usually it was something to do with the safety of the ship. You very rarely, on the ships I was on, got put in the brig for ordinary acts of foolishness, or pissing about. It was for smoking in forbidden quarters, which is a great hazard aboard a ship. It's stupid, yet you got blokes doing it. Or later on, when we was in action and we was in the Atlantic and we were searching for the big ones, I caught one bloke lighting a match – of all things – on deck. A lit match, even a glow of a cigarette is visible for several miles at sea, and don't forget, we was after the *Graf Spee*. These were the things where discipline was cracked down on. I myself was very, very strong about this.

I don't want to sound rotten about this, but in my opinion, having mixed with all parts of the other services, I would say the comradeship is highest in the navy

It's because it is the navy that the comradeship is the highest. It has to be. You have to trust one another. You usually sorted the bad ones out and they usually asked for a transfer or got transferred. The brotherhood was tightly knit. Obviously at times tempers got frayed – boredom, etcetera. Fights occurred, especially when you weren't in action, but after a bit you was all the best of mates. There was very few grudges carried. I carried one against an officer – I must admit this – because he was a homo. It wasn't being a homo that upset me so much but the fact he took advantage of very young ratings. I made his life such a bloody hell because I caught him red-handed. I had an idea this was going on. He got transferred in the end.

But you have to trust one another. I mean, I've seen lads like in submarines, in the old days you had to close them by hand (now they're sealed automatically) – all hatches are sealed in times of action. If you're in the parts that's flooded it's just too bloody bad. You drown, that's all there is to it. I've seen blokes go down hatches, like they did on the *Ajax*, and other boats where we've been in action, into hatches where the hatch had to be sealed after them, and they've known it's ten to one against them coming out of the hatch alive, and yet they've done it without flinching. I don't think it's bravery. It wasn't bravery – it was just that they knew that it was their job to do this, and the ship, and the rest of the men depended on them obeying their orders. I think a lot of them should have got V.C.'s. A lot of them never got mentioned – but it was this comradeship – you hesitated to obey the command.

There was no running to get into a bloody do that you had no chance of coming out of – let's get that right first of all

I was always afraid and I think if everybody would admit the truth – there wasn't such a word as cowardice – you was just shit scared of being the next one to cop it.

The *Ajax* was the flagship of the flotilla. It was supposed to be an attack flotilla because of all the torpedo tubes we were fitted out with. But you've got to get bloody near to a boat to fire these things – too bloody near, I'll tell you. And when you think we were being hit at fourteen mile away before we was anywhere near in range, and it wasn't shells they were firing, it was houses. Don't you believe that our navy had the edge on the German navy. Don't you believe it. Oh jeez – we had nothing, nothing to compare with. Even the very latest battleships –*King George Fifth, Prince of Wales* – they had fifteen inch guns but their fifteen inch guns couldn't compare with eleven inch guns the *Tirpitz* and *Graf Spee* had. One salvo from the main armament blew the bridge off our ship – several thousand tons, just as if it had never been there. All that was left was arms, legs, heads and a flood of blood. There wasn't a bit of metal left. There was one boat called the *Achilles* – if you had a double-decker 53 bus full of people you could have gone in and out of it. Fortunately every hole was above the water line, but they was literally right through the boat. You could see right through her. No. We had nothing.

I take my hat off to the Americans

Primarily they took a lot of our evacuees out of this country before the war got going; secondly they provided masses of food at very cheap rates, which was absolutely essential; then the armaments started flowing in; and then, when we started having terrible losses in shipping through the U boats, they started providing Liberty boats – the all welded, mass-produced boat, that was a real good cargo vessel. Don't listen to anyone who says they were a load of shit. They were as good as any other boat, and a lot of them are still in use to this very day. They was built with modern techniques, like the Germans used. We was lacking in this.

The Americans also gave our navy a lot of obsolete four funnelled destroyers. Right enough, they were obsolete – they was 1914 gear, but Christ, they weren't much worse for turn of speed or armaments than what our own were, and ours were supposed to be modern boats. They weren't much worse. They were heavier, they were a bit slower, a bit less manoeuvrable and they were sitting ducks for a fast raider like an E boat. E boats were all wood and extremely fast. They were fitted out with torpedo tubes and they used to come at you at 65 knots flat out – that's about 73, 74 mph – come out of the blue and BOOM! And you was left with four great steaming fish in you, and they was away. One of the latter uses of these American destroyers was for blocking port entrances such as Brest and Le Havre, and hazarding their shipping getting in and out. I don't agree with most of the people who say "Oh the Yanks were this, the Yanks were that." I take my hat off to the Yanks.

---

15 You went to war for six hours and you came back to clean sheets and ham and eggs

---

Waaf I was posted to Regents Park. It was ACR – Air Crew Receiving Centre – like for night vision and so on. They said to me "What do you want to do?" I said "I don't know what I want to do." First of all I was put down as an ACHGD[1] – that's anything. Like cleaning anything out. Then this officer, she said "There's a job here – you can either work in the cookhouse or you can work in sick quarters." I thought to myself: I don't fancy the cookhouse. So I said "I'll work in the sick quarters," even though the sight of blood made me faint.

I was in sick quarters a couple of days and I see a Waaf who I knew – Flo Ward. I knew Flo from before the war, because Mr Newton who had a furniture shop in the Barking Road used to be a tally man. She was his buyer. "Hallo Rene" she says. "Oh Flo" I said "I'm working in sick quarters. I can't stand it." "'Ere look Rene" she said "I'll put you wise. I'm doing typing and I know that they want postal clerks. Go in for that." "What can I do?" I said. "Look" she said "Don't put no make-up on – wash your face – and put on a sorrowful look and go and see the Waaf officer" ('cos I look sorrowful when I got no make-up, sallow like). I makes an appointment, don't I? I sees this Waaf officer. Left, right, left, right, left, right.

"Yes Airwoman, what do you want?" "I'm working in sick quarters Ma'am" I said. "It's making me feel ill. I can't stand it." "Yes, you do look rather ill" she said. "Is there a trade you want to go in for?" I thought: I'm alright here. "I would like to be a postal clerk" I said. She phones up and I had to report down the Post Office. Down I goes, and that's how I started doing the post office work. I did it all through the airforce.

I got away with murder myself, as far as discipline goes. I used to come home in civvies. I used to have silk stockings on. I was on a couple of charges, but I used to get out of it. Do you know who our Waaf officer was? Know Attlee?[2] His daughter. We used to have domestic night – one night a week you had to stop in and darn all your things and all that, and then you had to have a kit inspection. I was a rare one for walking about in me drawers – I never used to wear my trousers. My mate and me, we used to pluck each other's eyebrows and do our hair, and this Attlee, she used to say to me "Airwoman, every domestic night you're always improperly dressed." I thought: You right cow. Why shouldn't I walk around in me drawers?

Airgunner, Sergeant Before the war they might have seen the odd coloured people from the West Indies, but I don't think they had seen them in such great number. How can I put it? There wasn't – I don't know if you could call it prejudice – we had a lot of questions thrown at us. Different type of questions. Some people say "Where's your tail?"

In camp there was three stripe there, and whether they like it or not they had to respect it, but occasionally you hear

"I got away with murder myself, as far as discipline goes."

"Hallo Sambo" or another one he say "Eh, darkie" – "Snowball". All kinds of names. There were a few in the camps who kept themselves distant. You might have good friends in the camp – English friends – and when you go outside some of them act as if they don't want to know you. But then you get others, and you leave camp together and anywhere you go, they go. At the dances you get a little bit of jealousy, especially when you get to know most of the girls. At Henlow I get to know plenty of Waaf, and around Henlow you'd meet other girls, visit their houses, and they expect me to go and dance with them. You're dancing and all of a sudden somebody tap you on the shoulder and they say "Excuse me."

There were two very big Americans – white lads – that I knew well. They were stationed just outside Luton and we always meet when we go to Luton. We went to a pub one night – the regular pub we used to go into. We walk in and go to our table. We had another Jamaican lad with me but he was a much smaller lad, so he wants to show that he's as big as anybody else. He's first to order the drink. In comes three tremendously big Yanks, big white Yanks. They walk up to the bar, just as this feller is about to pick up his drink and walk back to the table.

This Yank just sweep the bar, swept off all the drinks, about six drinks off the bar. He said "Niggers are not allowed in here"

He didn't say anything. He re-ordered the drinks. They done the same thing again. The bartender – I think he was scared – he didn't want to get involved. Well, meself and the other Yanks and two girls was sitting at the table, and one of the white Yanks at the table, he's shouting "Re-order the drinks again."

He re-ordered and the bartender serve him the drinks. The Yank gets up from the table, walks over and stands behind this Jamaican lad. The other Yank means to do the same thing again, but this other Yank catch his hand and stopped him. He said "What do you want to do that for? His money's as good as yours." He said "Niggers are not allowed here." "What part of the States are you from?" He said "Texas." "How long have you been here?" "Oh" he said "we're just coming in." "Well" he said "Have you ever had to chase a bullet up your backside?" These Yanks at our table had just come back from the Front. They just get their leave, and these others are coming straight from America. "If you want to see the wound, it's here." He said "I didn't know it was your friends." "Yes, they are my friends, and you'll pay for those drinks you tipped over." He said "What's the damage?" and paid for the drinks.

I was an airgunner but all the time I was on stand-by. It might sound funny, but that's the one regret I have. I never went on an operation.

Bomb Aimer After you'd finished your training they put you in a big room – fifty pilots, fifty navigators, fifty air bombers, a hundred airgunners, fifty engineers – and they let you mix for a couple of days. Then they came in and said "Who's the crews?" and they marked them all down. I don't know how the other crews picked themselves, but I know how we picked ourselves. We were all Scotsmen.

MacNamara came up to me and said "I've got a feller from Aberdeen in the rear turret and a feller from Galashiels in the mid upper, do you fancy joining us?" "Aye, alright." Being aircrew you all had to be reasonably intelligent, so that was different – everything was different in aircrew – the whole set-up. You went to war for six hours and you came back to clean sheets and when you did an operation you got ham and eggs. No one else did.

I never dropped a bomb in my life

We were a protection society for the rest of the main force – try to kid the Germans on the main force wasn't coming their way. It was a hell of a job. One of the things we had to do was go up to 20,000 feet and circle for six hours round our own arse. Round and round and round. We had three wireless operators in the aircraft and they jammed the radar of the Germans, so you had a complete screen from Denmark to France. The idea was that when the main force broke through the screen the Germans only had time from the coast to the target to get their fighters up. Oh, but that was agony.

The first time someone shot at us – and they happened to be Americans – I got the fright of my life. I was in the foetal position, making myself as small as I can. I looked at my mate Eddie and said "For fuck's sake, let's no do this any more. It's alright for a joke, but let's chuck it now." I would normally have been an airbomber, but in this group we had no bombs to drop, so I became second pilot, second airgunner, second everything. I was running up and down the plane like a blue-arsed fly. The only thing the crew hoped was that I wasn't the second pilot when the pilot died. I used to fly it home and they'd say "For Christ's sake, you're making us seasick."

I enjoyed my first flight. I really did enjoy it

Flight Engineer I was a right sproggy. I hadn't done any flying whatsoever. So I get in and there were two instructors. One for the pilot and one for the engineer. They're called screen pilot and screen engineer. They cover you, in fact. My instructor

"Nobody could explain to you what flying on an Op was like. Nobody could really tell you what to expect."

really looked old to me – he must have been all of 30! He said "My God, they must be robbing the bloody cradles!" I was 20.

After not many hours – six in fact – we were fit enough to go out on our own. They loaded you up with a heap of dummy bombs and they send you out on what they call a loaded climb. We were then posted to Mildenhall, to a squadron. The Flight Commander took Jack, the pilot, and I up – just the two of us, to see how we coped on Stirlings. He passed us as being fit for flying on Ops. Then they suddenly decided that we were going to convert to Lancasters. The conversion course was a matter of hours. This was at Thetford in Norfolk. We were now ready to fly Ops.

Nobody could explain to you what flying on an Op was like. Nobody could really tell you what to expect. Jack had done one trip, just before our first Op, called a "second dicky". He got taken out to be shown what it was like. The rest of us hadn't done any operational flying at all. When we were ready to fly we had a lecture from a chappie who had escaped from a German prison. He'd got back to this country, like many other airman. We were escape orientated. We all carried escape kits:

compasses and so on – not because the RAF were doing us a favour, but because we'd cost so much to train that we were supposed to try and get back.

The first trip was to Essen and I must admit, I was dead scared. Every time I saw a great big bright light I shut my eyes. If I'd only known it was the easiest trip we ever had, or were ever likely to get. It was a very very cloudy night and all these bright lights I kept seeing were the reflections of bombs flashing back on the clouds, or searchlights playing under clouds. I was supposed to keep a log every 15 minutes – logging engine temperature of four engines, logging oil temperature, speed, boost – a heap of stuff. Well, you don't. You don't want to know. It was a big laugh when I went back next morning and I said I'd lost my log book, because obviously they knew – first time out, everybody lost their log!

The second trip we did was Nuremburg, which was the worst air battle of the lot – but we didn't know that did we? We had nothing to compare it with

It was a running battle from the time we crossed the Channel. We didn't know, though, that this was unusual. Other crews would, but this was only our second trip. By the time we got to Nuremburg we were shattered. You didn't need a navigator. You could navigate by the combats going on ahead of you and by the aircraft burning on the ground. We were shattered. There's no other word for it. We hadn't lost our morale – we were all doing our jobs – but we were scared. Dead scared. We had logged 32 aircraft going down until Jack said "Pack it up." I remember him swearing at a Lancaster which was going down in flames – he wanted it to blow up because the longer it kept in flames the easier it was for other people to see us. Jack was normally a mild sort of man. We buckled our parachutes on, which I never did ever again.

We took a vote because the rear turret wouldn't work, whether we should turn back or not. It was the skipper's decision, but he always reckoned that as we were flying as a crew we should vote. We all voted to go on. Over the target two Junkers 88s attacked us. We were sitting ducks. The wireless operator got down on his hands and knees and prayed to Christ. He had his intercom on, and it came over on the intercom. Who knows? It might have had some effect because they sheared off and shot down people either side of us.

Back we had a quiet trip. Sharma the navigator, who was a crack navigator, reckoned we were over Brest, which was a heavily defended area. There was a hell of a lot of searchlights which made us think it was Brest. We got quite a scare. We were busy shoving out "Window", the stuff that puts their radar off, and we had a gadget which messed their searchlights up. It had no effect on them whatsoever.

We thought, any minute now they're going to open up and blow us out of the sky

I'd let a tank run dry – which shows what a state we were in panicwise – and had trouble restarting the engine, and that engine ran the radar set. Suddenly the searchlights started to-ing and fro-ing, and it was Manston, Kent. Not Brest at all. I always remember feeling – I don't know what the word is . . . Because besides anything else we were almost out of fuel. The winds we had been told to expect were wrong, and we had been flying against headwinds.

Manston was not only a fighter base but also an emergency landing space for bombers. You could get several aircraft down at once in that place. As we were coming in to land there was a chappie behind us and he was listing what was wrong with his aircraft. Terrible things – he couldn't get his wheels down; he had so much shot away from behind; he had so many crew members dead – I thought "Christ Almighty, what have we got to complain about?"

Nuremburg took us six hours forty-five minutes, from take-off to return. Lots of people used to reckon the Germans knew we were coming. It seemed obvious, but I can't really believe the allegations that they had been informed by our own Intelligence. You wouldn't have sent that many aircraft would you? Seven hundred was a hell of a size force. You'd have sent a smaller force. They've slain this book that says the Nuremburg raid was leaked.[3] They say his facts are all up the creek. But we were really shattered. We thought if it was going to be like this, we haven't got a chance in hell. As it happens, we were one of the few crews in our squadron to complete a tour.

Before an Op there were rituals like weeing on the tail-wheel, and you'd joke such as "You haven't got a chance in hell tonight with your lot" or "You'll find that bloody aircraft won't see you back for breakfast" or "You're for the chop tonight". It was said all the time, even if someone was killed. You just carried on. If you didn't joke there was dead quietness. In the American airforce you could suffer from what was called "Combat Fatigue". In the airforce you suffered from Lack of Moral Fibre, which was stamped all across your paybook, all your documents – LMF, and you're stripped of your rank. And this could lead to trouble because you might have a crew member who was going round the twist and in doing so was endangering the rest of the crew. You couldn't pack it in and say "I don't want to fly anymore, please", could you? We were dead scared but on our third trip I don't think we thought "I wonder what's going to happen to us."

Towards the end of my tour we started doing daylights over France. The buzz bombs and the V2's were getting bad and our targets were the various V2 bases. I was astounded to see field after field pitted with bombholes. This was before our troops had got that far. There didn't seem to be a field in France that wasn't pox-marked with craters.

On the 26 June 1945 we took our groundcrew over Germany, to show them what they'd helped us to do. What we called Cooks Tour. We went from the flooded areas of Holland to Cologne, from Cologne to Bonn, from Bonn to Mainz, Frankfurt, Dortmund, Düsseldorf, Duisburg, Essen, Wuppertal, Wesel – which was nothing left at all, as I remember – Arnhem, Nijmegen, Rotterdam and back to base. What I saw I thought was disgusting.

Cologne was just rubble. The railway station was like Paddington, but all you could see were the arches. The Cathedral was standing right next door to it – the spire was still standing. It looked reasonably whole but apart from that you couldn't see a building standing. All the bridges were down or seemed to be. At Frankfurt I saw a hospital, like a U sideways.

It had great Red Crosses on the roof. One wing was completely gutted and the other one had bomb holes in it.

Obviously you can't see what you're bombing at night, but according to our propaganda it was only the Germans who bombed hospitals

The only time when we were on Ops I can remember about people as such, as distinct from cities and industries, was when we were going to Essen. Our Intelligence Officer was giving us all the old madam and then he said "You'll be arriving when they're changing shifts." That was about the only time I ever thought exactly what we were going to do. We were not only going to bomb a factory and its plant, we were also going to bomb two lots of work people, and among those work people were probably Russians, French, apart from Germans. He actually mentioned "People", instead of aiming points, which was usual. People weren't talked of. It was aiming points and targets. You didn't think, did you? It was orientated that way.

---

[1] Aircraft Hand – General Duties.
[2] Clement Attlee. Labour Prime Minister, 1945–1951.
[3] *The Nuremburg Raid* by Martin Middlebrook, Allen Lane.

---

16 Last night's action was bordering on mutiny

RAF Electrician The conditions in Gibraltar were really bloody horrible. In the nighttime we were sleeping on petrol cans, in the day there was the levanter – a sort of steam on top of the Rock, which at night used to come down and you got absolutely bloody soaked. It was like being in a vapour bath. When you woke up in the morning and the sun came out you were sweating, so you couldn't get dry. You got terrible dysentery, and with the flies and whatnot it was bleeding

"As Station Electrician I could skive."

horrible. The result was that the M.O. wouldn't guarantee the health of anybody who stayed more than 18 months. So the tour of duty was 18 months. Afterwards you got sent home. All the previous draft on Gib had been sent home after 18 months. It was so bad that blokes used to throw themselves off the Rock.

As time went on they didn't do much about blokes' quarters, but they gradually put concrete over the race course. They turned it into a proper runway, to take more heavier things. Then, something was in the air. They started to import Spitfires, boxed in crates. Blokes were assembling them, working right through. They worked two, three days at a stretch, with hardly any sleep. I was lucky. As Station Electrician I could skive. Eventually it broke: The African Campaign –Montgomery's victory. Terrific cheers. At last a breakthrough. Everybody's looking forward to going home – some of them only had a couple of months to go. Then, all of a sudden, a notice is posted on the DRO's:[1] "As a result of the African Victory the tour of duty in Gibraltar has been increased to 18 months in Gibraltar, followed by 18 months in Africa." The blokes just couldn't believe it. Some of them were just about to go home.

Before they did, they took the sparking plug out of the fire-engine. They were saying "We're not tolerating this. We didn't work our bollocks off for this." It was a spontaneous reaction. Then the lads in our camp, the land base, they discussed it. "What shall we do?" "Let's not go to work tomorrow. Let's have a strike." Most of them thought they were a bit daft at the Seaplane camp, 'cos they were really sticking their necks out.

The officers were dead quiet. Not a word. This was in all camps – including the radio camp on top of the Rock. They were all discussing it. Nobody went to work the next day. Well, very very few. Eventually the officers realised it was getting out of hand, so they put up on the DROs "We recognise that the decision to extend the tour of duty was very unpopular, and therefore we have decided to form an answer back committee. Officers will be present in the canteen and any airman who cares to come along can ask questions. All formalities will be waived. You can ask whatever questions you like. There will be no disciplinary action taken."

We went along to this meeting. The CO got up. "Look" he said "I feel just as bad about this as you do. I've made representations to the Air Ministry to tell them how bad people feel about this. I'm waiting for a reply. Meanwhile, whilst we're waiting, there's no reason why things couldn't be made a bit easier. If any of you have any suggestions or any questions . . ." We kept on for a little while about the 18 months tour of duty. Is it fair, etcetera. The CO said "I can't reply to this one. I've made my protest to the Air Ministry. I'm waiting for a reply. Now anything else?"

"Why can't we have decent conditions to live in?" "We'll see to that." "We think it disgusting that in weather like this not to have sheets or pyjamas. Can we have some issued?" "Yes, you can have that issued." And we complained also about the canteen.

Not very long before this happened an incident occurred where the officers had a dance. There was no women on the Rock so they got the Wrens from the Naval Base. There were a few there, but you hardly ever saw them. Before the officers had their dance they got the lads – who didn't know what was going on – to put sackcloth all around the officers' mess and they made it out of bounds. The dance occurred and the Wrens came in. And the penny dropped – "Oh boy! What a shower of bastards!" They were really resentful.

At this answer back committee one of the chaps says "I think, sir, we ought to have a dance." "Dance?" "Yes!" "Who are you going to dance with?" "You had the Wrens along here, didn't you? We'll have them along here, to dance with us" "But there's so many of you and we've only got a few Wrens!" "Alright, we'll have Excuse-me dances, all the way along." They postponed their decision until the next answer back committee, but we had our dance. You've never seen anything like it! A dozen Wrens and 200 blokes excuse-me dancing all the time! Mind you, I don't know what all the fuss was about. They were real bloody crabs. A snooty, middle-class lot.

As a result of our action they compromised and cut the tour of duty down to two years. They also built a rest camp on the Rock. Another result of the mutiny was that some lads were allowed to go to Tangiers, after they'd done 18 months on the Rock. By the way, they held the NCOs responsible for any further acts of mutiny. Although a terrific amount of damage was done no one was charged, as far as I know.

The only thing in Gib was a main street with umpteen pubs. Booze was dirt cheap and you could get pissed as a newt. Lots of them became alcoholics because of that. To make matters worse, all the civilians – the women, children and old people – had been evacuated. The Gibraltarians. They had been evacuated to England. There was no women. They used to import Spanish labour for the shops. They used to come in from across the border. They didn't work in the camps, of course.

I could speak Spanish and I got to know one or two people who claimed they were working for the Spanish Underground

One bloke in town, he used to work in a typewriter shop and was always talking about "Viva La Republica" and all the rest of it, but he wasn't very political. But there was a girl who worked in a tobacco shop I used to go in. She was very political and very interested in working against Franco. One day, when she got to know me sufficiently well, she gave me a text. "There's an underground movement in Spain and we'd like to have this duplicated. Do you know anyone who can duplicate this?" It was asking that women who were prisoners of Franco should be allowed to have milk, and that prisoners in general should be allowed to have books. I said to her "I don't think much of that." "You've got to start with small things. You've got to get the sympathy of the population. We feel it would be a useful exercise."

I took the text and went to the feller who was always talking about the "Republica" in the typewriter shop. "Tell me, what do you think of this?" He read it. "Marvellous! Where'd you get it from?" "Never mind where I got it from – can you duplicate some?" "Certainly. What's it for?" "It'll be taken into Spain." "With the greatest of pleasure. Come back on Tuesday. I'll have them ready for you."

I went back on the Tuesday and the chap says "Here you are, here's your duplicated leaflet." And standing there is a soldier. "Hey" I said "perhaps he can understand Spanish." "Yes, he can. I'll introduce you to him. So and so and so and so, Corporal, member of the Security Police!" I thought: bloody hell! He shakes hands with me. "Pleased to meet you. That's a very good leaflet you have there." I says "Yeah, as a matter of fact I wanted a few to send to my friends, who'd be interested in what's going on in Spain. I couldn't tell him I wanted half a dozen, so I told him to print a few more."

"Don't give us a cock and bull story like that. I know they're going into Spain. Who's taking them in?" "Nobody's taking them in." "Don't kid be. Don't get be wrong – this is a good leaflet. It's useful." "How do you mean – useful?" "Well, we know for an absolute fact that Franco is sending wolfram (a stuff required for making steel) to Germany. If we have leaflets like this we can get to know people in the underground and if we can tell Franco who they are, we can have some bargaining power with him. You want to see the war won, don't you?" I took my bloody time. I said "If I could help you, I would."

"Perhaps we'll take them in." "You do what you like with them." In fact, he allowed me to keep them. I went back to camp, got rid of the bloody things and decided not to go back to the girl. A friend of mine, a Scots laddie, went and tipped her off.

A couple of weeks later, in the middle of the night, they suddenly woke me up. "You're being posted"

"What?" "You're being posted. Pack your kit. We're going in two hours." "Where?" "Sorry, can't tell you." I packed my kit and thought: What the bloody hell? I didn't even have a chance to say good-bye to anyone. They took me out, onto a boat, right out into the Med and then they transferred me to another boat. When I got on the boat there was a whole lot of RAF blokes – and they're all yellow! They told me they had come from Takoradi in the Gold Coast and they'd been taking mepacrin tablets against malaria, which made them yellow. They also told me that we were on our way home. I thought: Marvellous!

On the boat were all services – navy, army, and airforce. The conditions were really rotten. Every night an announcement used to come on the tannoy that went something like this: "The time is now 2100 hours. All other ranks will go below decks. Officers and first class passengers may remain on deck until 2200 hours. Please extinguish your cigarettes." This was standard, apparently, on all troop ships, and of course it really got up bloke's noses.

On the boat I came across a bloke who'd taught me to play the trumpet as a kid. He'd been to the Gold Coast and was in this RAF band which was aboard. Every evening the band used to go into a room and entertain the blokes. One day one of the band came along and said "We're on jankers. The CO called us into the office and said we had to play for the officers and first class passengers, and that there wouldn't be a concert for the lads tonight. We told him we're a RAF band, and don't think it's right." "Right," he said "You're all on jankers and there'll be no concert at all tonight."

The story got round – "Bleeding bastards!" That night the

blokes decided they were going to occupy this bloody room.
We were going to have our own party. We crowded in and
didn't allow anyone else in and we started to put on a concert –
singing songs like *Eskimo Nell*, telling dirty jokes and things
like that. The funniest thing was, I think the officers and first
class passengers must have had a better time than if the band
had played, because they were all outside, looking through the
windows, absolutely killing themselves with laughter. We had
the most marvellous evening.

And then, the stupid bastards, they went and did the
announcement over the tannoy "It is now 2100 hours . . ."
They couldn't have been more tactless. A howl went up and
they all burst out on deck, all these yellow faces. They'd been
drinking, as well. "The rotten sods!" "We'll throw the CO in
the sea!" and they started singing the *Red Flag* and the
Internationale. Then, through the tannoy: "Will all ranks go
below decks" – "Fuck you, you rotten bastards, we're not
going below decks" they shouted back. It was murder! It went
on till about 1 o'clock in the morning. They let it fade out
gradually. Everyone drifted down. Everybody felt really good.

Next morning all the NCO's were called in to see the CO.
One of them comes back – "Look lads" he says "they've made
us personally responsible for another occurrence. We're all
going to be put on a charge." "We'll stand by you, if they put
you on a charge. They won't put you on a charge." The lads
still wanted to carry on with it. The NCO's were called in again.
The CO asked them to assemble all the lads down below decks.
Everybody's down there, all ranks, all services. In fact, the
airforce and the navy were the most militant – the army wasn't,
funnily enough. In walks the Adjutant. He comes marching
along. All of a sudden there's a snigger. "Shut up!" – Really
"SHUT UP!" He's pacing backwards and forwards like a
bloody, bleeding rat. Backwards and forwards. Then suddenly
the CO comes in. There are more sniggers and the Adjutant is
really screaming "SHUT UP! SHUT UP!"

**The CO's walking backwards and forwards – "Last night's action
was bordering on mutiny!" And they pissed themselves laughing!**

The Adjutant's going mad. "SHUT UP! SHUT UP!" The CO says "I don't understand what all the discontent is all about. After all, you've all had good food" – More guffaws of laughter – "Isn't the food good? You've had fruit!" The chaps were laughing. The Adjutant's going "SHUT UP! SHUT UP!" and eventually quietens them down. "Why – haven't you had any fruit? – Have you had any fruit?" he says to this chappie. "Well, sir, I've had one small apple." "And the food's been good, hasn't it?" "No sir." And the Adjutant says "Don't answer back!" "Well, all I'm saying to you is this, I can promise you all any further action like this and the whole lot of you will be arrested as soon as we dock in England." The lads were dismissed.

They went on talking though, and there didn't seem any sign that it was abating, so they stopped the boat there and then. There, where it was. Just stopped. Dead silence. Nobody knew what was happening. Nobody knew what to do. They kept it like that for nearly a day. Then they said "Start unloading the hold. Get your kits ready. We'll soon be landing." We didn't know where the hell we were. The boat started to move, and we discovered that we were off the coast of Ireland. Eventually we came to somewhere near Morecambe and disembarked. And that was the end of it.

---

[1] Daily Routine Orders.

17

A lot of my troubles came about almost naturally when I met the same attitudes in the British army as I had been learning about in fascism

Fusilier During the army I had about 27 cases of absence, countless charges of disobedience, insubordination, dumb insolence, inciting mutiny, escapes from prison and escorts and

two or three court martials. Most of this didnae came about
because I didnae want to fight, or because I was a conscientious
objector – indeed, in the beginning I joined the army because I
thought it was the only way to fight fascism. A lot of my
troubles came about almost naturally when I met the same
attitudes in the British army as I had been learning about in
fascism. Mind you, the problem of absenteeism and desertion
was so great that one of the best known slogans of the war was
"You Can't Spell Victory With An Absentee", and to combat
it they had special squads of military police and civilian police
who were used in an attempt to round up the men and women
on the run.

In Glasgow they raided places like St Vincent Street, where
they had a mobile coffee stall. Quite regular the squads
would raid such places in an attempt to pick up deserters.
Sometimes this meant quite innocent people – disabled people,
wounded people, people on leave – were picked up and taken
into custody to be checked. If the Gestapo came to Britain
there certainly would have been a lot of candidates amongst
some of the civilian cops that I met.

You never deserted without taking all your kit, and looking
smart. That was the system. I used to travel up and down the
country regular for nothing You took your rifle and bayonet,
your gas mask and your helmet. You walked into a station.
You knew most of the time MPs would stop you and you
wouldnae get on the platform with the ticket inspector. So the
secret was to take the bull by the horns. Walk up to the MP and
say "I'm Fusilier Morrison. I'm with an escort. Did you see a
Corporal here in the same regiment as me go onto the train?"
And they would say "I'm no so sure Jock. He might have went
on. Away in and look." You walked in and climbed onto the
train. You'd say the same thing to the ticket inspector. Once
you were on the train, that was it.

When ever the inspector came round you said the same
thing. "We're in an escort and the Corporal went away ahead.
We thought he was on the train, but we cannae find him
anywhere. He must have gone on a train before." He'd say
"You're on an escort. Fair enough. What's your name
anyway?" Take your name. And that was it, and if you were

really brassnecked, just tell them you were absent – bluntly. "I'm going back to my unit." "Where's your unit?" "My unit's in such and such a place." "OK, that's fair enough." And that was you. Another one was, if you met an ATS, go into the toilet with her and when he came round, and came to the door, let her pass her ticket out underneath. In they days they were nae as permissive in their thinking as they are today. These were the ways we travelled all over the place.

Some of my worst experiences were in India. A small group of us – privates and a Corporal – had been in a hill station and we all decided to go back to camp a day early and visit a place called Muttra. We'd been there before. It was a brothel. I didnae want to go back and neither did some of the others. It was old hat to us, but some did, particularly the Corporal. We got to the foot of the hills and because of a landslide the train was late. Another train turned up and the NCO was determined to get to his brothel.

The train that came was an old tumbledown shackle thing that the Indians used to use – betel nut spit all over the floor. The Corporal saw the RTO – the transport officer. He says to him "Can I get a compartment cleared out for the lads, because we want to take this train." I said to the transport officer, a sergeant "We're not due back until a certain time. If we catch the morning train we'll be back in time. Is that OK?" He said "Yes."

"Well, we're refusing to take this train. We want to take the next one. Besides, we don't fancy going into these compartments with all the betel nut and all the rest of it." But the Corporal was determined. They held the train up. There was seven of us who refused. The Corporal gets the rations and puts them on the train with the help of some privates who decided to go. Then he says to us "I'm asking you once: are you going to follow the rations?" That's one of the things that makes it an order – you're supposed to go where the rations go.

"Are you going to follow the rations?" "No." "Two: are you going to follow the rations?" "No." "Three: are you going to follow the rations?" We were a wee bit hesitant. He'd told us he was going to give us three chances. We gave an explanation why we were nae going to go – to keep it as evidence. "Are you going to follow the rations?" "No." That's it. They went on the train. The train pulled away. We went to the RTO, got our passes signed, saying why we had done it, and that if we get in on time we wouldn't be classed as absent.

As luck may have it, we were late. The train was late and we reported ten minutes after our passes were up. The Corporal, apparently, hadnae got to his brothel, which meant he'd got back to the camp in Delhi early. He was annoyed, so he put in a charge against us. As soon as we came into the camp we were put into the guardroom. Taken out in the morning, charged, and put in front of the Company Commander. The Sergeant-Major who marches us in said "Where is your evidence? Where are your passes?" Foolishly, we handed them over, and they disappeared.

The Company Commander got our explanation, and without any further chance to explain, he told us that he was giving us seven days CB for being late – absent without leave. We refused his punishment. We asked to see the Commanding Officer, which we were entitled to do. He asked us if we were prepared to accept his punishment, after trying us. We said "No" and we were remanded for court martial, the charge now being "Inciting Mutiny" against me, being the oldest soldier. I had led the other six young soldiers into refusing to obey an order.

I lay in prison for seven month, along with everybody else – without even being tried! The padre came up regular (this is where I took a dislike to padres) and pleaded with me to give in. Mind you, if I'd accepted seven days CB I'd have been out. They were all saying "Give in" and making threats about never seeing our mothers again, but the principle was more important to us, and we stuck it out.

In between that time we seen things that I'd never hope to see again

We were in a compound that was surrounded by barbed wire. At that time the First Battalion Royal Scots Fusiliers had the biggest police force that I've ever seen in a unit I've been in. The reason for that was as follows. Delhi cantonment – the camp we were in – had what they called an invisible perimeter. The Indians used to herd their cattle around it, and sometimes into it. From time to time the cattle would stray onto our cantonment. The Battalion HQ Quarter-Master Sergeant-Major had a notice put up in every dining room in the camp, informing all fusiliers, which we were, that if they found these animals straying into our property it was our duty to bring them to the Quarter-Master's stores, or to the battalion cookhouse for slaughter. Right. That is the situation.

When I was imprisoned in this compound I discovered that the police acted as rustlers. They used to go outside and force the cattle in, under the authority of the Sergeant-Major who was in charge of the police. They'd collect the money for the cattle they'd rustled, and then when the cowman came looking for his cattle, into the perimeter, they whipped him into prison. They stripped him of everything – looted all his stuff, gave him nothing and left him there. They wouldn't give him a place to shit. They done that with us too, by the way. They done this until the poor wee guy was crying to get out – and I mean grovelling – to get out.

And then they would form themselves into a gauntlet, with their truncheons and sticks, and the man would have to run through the rank. The rank was never under twenty and sometimes nearer thirty men. He'd run down, getting slaughtered – slaughtered – as he went out. Rarely ever came back. I seen that happen time without number.

With us, we'd get sent out with prisoners who had already been tried, to what they called the maidan. It's an open space, and the police, or whoever was in charge of you, would sit under a tree. It was like an American chain-gang. They used to have us cutting grass with the edge of the shovel in the height of the sun when the Indians and everybody else were kipping it up, from 2 o'clock to 4 o'clock. That's what they had us doing. I've seen men with the skin literally raised off their back, and the blood's running out of them, the blood caked up and dried.

You've probably heard the tales of picking the sand up, bits of sand up – that's true – and guys sadistically standing over you. Wouldnae even give you a drink. Men collapsing and the guy coming along with a bucket of water and throwing it over

That's a fact. There's no shenanigan about that. That all
happened. They done it to me.

In the meantime my hair had grown fairly long, and the
Sergeant-Major decided that I was to get a haircut. I always
stuck by the rules, as I seen them. It was only when they pushed
that wee bit from the other side that I started to kick and I
really kicked. "Get a haircut." So I decided to get the first
haircut. They took me out of my cell. It was an Indian. He cut
my hair. Made quite a nice job of my hair, and that was it.

The Sergeant-Major came along in the morning and said
"Right, turn round Morrison, let's see your back." Turned
round – I was always regimental – everything was done military
style, in drill. "Oh that's nae use. You'll need to get more off."
Anger creeping in. Following morning, out again. More off.
Without dragging the story out, it took about three days,
maybe four days until I was only left with one tuft of hair on the
top of my head. One bit. My patience is getting tried. "That's
the end of it," I said to myself. I asked the Orderly Officer who
came round the cells at night "Sir, do you think I need a
haircut?" "No." It was obvious I didnae. "The Sergeant-Major
has said I've got to get a haircut." "In that case Morrison, if
that's what Sergeant-Major says, you've got to get it. Get the
man out for another haircut." The corporals know me and
they said "The barber will not be around till tomorrow."
Sympathy was beginning to grow up, with certain people. The
officer says "Have him out for a haircut tomorrow."

**"What do I do now Walter?" That's what I said to myself. "What
do I do now?"**

I searched round about the cell. I was in a cell about nine feet
long and roughly about my arms width, with a wooden bed and
a pail. That was me. I'd done a big drawing of myself on the
wall, and I used to box it, shadow-box it, to keep myself fit, and
to let them see there was no mug in the cell. I happened to see
on top of the cell doors, which were iron railings, an iron bar
attached to the railings with screws, and on top of that was
sharp rusty spikes. Besides the cell doors were storm doors that

came in to keep the sandstorms from blowing in. When the police went off at night the military guard came on and I says to the guy "Will you shut my storm door?"

He closed the storm door and I unscrewed this iron bar and managed to get it off, which meant I was left with a gladiator-type weapon which I managed to hide. First thing in the morning the Orderly officer comes around again to inspect the guard, and he comes round the cells to take anybody who wants to go on the sick. I had it all planned out. I asked to go and see the Medical Officer, which to me seemed the logical step because I was not only wanting to ask him about my hair being any shorter, but I was now being affected mentally, and I couldnae see any other way that I could have this brought out into the open. If anything happened I wanted references back. They took me over.

I says "Sir, I'm here to see you about my hair." There was a notice up in the battalion that because of the sun you'd only to get your hair cut to a certain length. "The situation's this sir – I've been told to get another haircut." "If Sergeant-Major says so, you've got to get it done." That's one thing about the army – you can be the biggest villain under the sun and they just throw their weight behind each other. "Well sir, if anybody comes into my cell to take me to get another bit of hair cut off, I'll kill them on the spot. The reason I've come to you, sir, is that I'm hoping you'll take it seriously, because if I do it, then you being a medical man you should understand people's minds, and you'll be held responsible. I'm telling you – it's going to happen." I went on about how I've been trained by the army to fight for what I think's right: that I knew how to kill people, and that this seemed like a time I was going to have to do it.

Christ! They were shitting themselves. I had a name that if I said it, they knew I would do it. They took me back to my cell. Now by this time – you take it from me – the place was buzzing – "Hear Morrison's doing this" – "Hear Morrison's doing that." Everybody in the unit knew. It's getting nearer and nearer the time for the barber to come. Talk about *High Noon*! *High Noon* was nothing on it. I'm sitting there with this iron bar, getting worried and worried and worried. I'm saying

"What if it's big Jimmy that comes in? What if it's so and so?
I'll have to kill them." Take it from me – it was there to be done.
The first person that would have come in my cell would have
copped it.

Would you believe my cell door wasnae opened for – och – I
was going to say seven days – I cannae remember the thing, because everything became such a "Where am I? – What have I
done?" that I don't remember. But it wasnae that day, and it
wasnae the next day, and all the food was fed through the bars
to me. The piss was running over the top of my bucket and they
wouldnae let me out for a shit, but I never had another piece of
hair taken from my head. The lesson from that was, for me –
Oh Christ, I don't want to be in that position again because I
would have killed some poor bugger. That's what turned me to
pacifism, actually.

**After months and months of sitting in jail we were finally taken
before the Commanding Officer**

We were waiting on confirmation of the Brigadier's report on
the Court Martial. Everybody seen me getting sent away for
years. The padre came round asking, would he say a prayer for
me? The seven of us were taken up in front of the Commanding
Officer and marched in. Everybody was in front of me, then I
was taken in. I was given 156 days detention, as I was picked
out as the ringleader. The rest of them got, we'll say in the
region of 28 days field punishment. We're marched out.
"Prisoners and escort – caps on!" We put our caps on. I said
"What's on now?" "Quick march!" Back in again. The
Commanding Officer: "In the case of Private Morrison, blah,
blah, blah, although you have been given such and such, blah,
blah, blah, the Brigadier has failed to confirm your sentence,
and you will be released immediately." So we won, in a
roundabout way. I was released, given some leave and all my
back-pay.

That night I went to the garrison theatre to see a film. There
was a big searchlight shining into the place where we all stood
queuing, waiting to get into the pictures. Big lines of all the
lads, and the padre comes up on his bicycle. He comes up to

me. "Morrison, can I speak to you." "Yes. What is it?" "I want to congratulate you on your release and on your stand." "Away to fuck, you of little faith. I don't need your help or anybody else's." And all the boys are going "Whe-heyy!" How can you have faith in people like that? They talk about a guy called Christ that's no prepared to surrender certain things and yet, when it comes to the crunch, they're pleading with me to give in.

Private I had been in a graded battalion because I only had one good eye and also because my father was never naturalised. Graded battalions were attached to various infantry regiments. I went into the Gloucesters, then I was transferred to the Wiltshire Regiment, back to the Gloucesters, from there into the Green Howards and I finally ended up in the Royal Army Ordinance Corps. Not only was I fed up with all this shunting around but I was also frustrated at the pettiness of army life and, quite honestly, I wanted to get out of the army. I wanted to get away.

I was eventually sent to a selection centre. They had people from all over – from different units – for various reasons, medical, psychological, whatever. They were sent to the Selection Centre to be sorted out and sent to more suitable units. This was at Aberystwyth. It was a great big unit, based on the town, with teams of psychiatrists to sort all these oddballs out.

My papers didn't arrive with me. They got lost, somehow. So instead of doing the usual 14 days of routine inspections, testings and then finally being posted, I was there for 28 days, by which time I was thoroughly pissed off. Incidentally, about 35 to 40 per cent passing through this centre were given their tickets. They were just useless.

I was in a genuinely serious nervous condition. In fact I was being given luminol. At the same time, which was an expression of the same thing, I had developed piles. This was around Christmas. Having been told not to go sick or else I'd be charged with malingering, I asked for an interview with the Commanding Officer, and I got it. I explained the predicament. I want to go sick, but if I do I'm told I'll be charged with malingering. He arranged immediately for a special sick report

When I arrived there, there was a lance corporal – a medical orderly – and he had this bit of paper in his hand, which was the special sick report. I waited for the doctor to arrive. It was Boxing Day. I'd been down in the dumps for a couple of days and the blokes had persuaded me to come to this bloody Christmas do. I had probably eaten too much and the piles really came on. I was bleeding and I was in a nervous state. The Medical Officer on duty happened to be one of the psychiatrists who I understand, though I'm not sure, was filling in for someone else. He came into the room and during a short conversation between him and the medical orderly I heard him saying something like (because on every form there is your religion) "Oh these bloody people are all the same" – so I could tell straight away he was anti-semitic. He turned to me and started to abuse me. "I know you buggers, I'll have you on a charge", and all this. I said "Hadn't you better examine me before you start making all these accusations?" He said "Yes! I will! – Get undressed!" And as I turned he shoved me in the back.

Well, I turned round and all hell was let loose. I really went for him. I finished up on the floor, with one bloke kneeling on my neck, one on each of my limbs

I'm stretched out, practically unconscious. They even started to interrogate me, but they decided to sit me on a chair and give me a cigarette. They let me go, so I went for him again. Well, that was it. They calmed me down. They gave me treatment for my piles, so there was no question of having been a malingerer. That bit was dropped completely. Next morning I'm for Company Orders – I'm on a charge for striking a superior officer. I explained all the circumstances and they said "If your allegations are true it's still no defence. You complain about the misbehaviour of your superiors, you don't strike them." I was charged and remanded in custody, pending a court martial, because it was a court martial charge.

I was kept in close arrest, the term being close arrest, not custody. I was marched through the town three times a day under escort, for my meals to the cookhouse. I had to parade every day for Company Orders, for 24 hour remands. This went on for six weeks. I was visited by a rabbi towards the end, who half suggested to me that if I would agree to a report to the effect that I wasn't really responsible for my actions, that I might make an easy case of it. I said "If anybody wants to say that, they're welcome to, but don't expect me to agree with them."

They sent me to see a psychiatrist. I managed, on the way back under escort, to find out the contents of the report – which is a normal thing in the army. You very seldom travel with documents relating to yourself that you don't try somehow to find out the contents, which I did do. In fact I objected to the use of the psychiatrist's report because in all the answers to the questions, set by the convenors of the court martial, were traps. Like "Will this man suffer from, or benefit from punishment". And he said "Neither." All that sort of thing, so I wouldn't have a bloody chance.

To cut the story short, this carried on for six weeks before the court martial was actually convened because I kept refusing to have any representation. I wanted to conduct the defence myself, and then I discovered through the regimental police sergeant that there was an officer in the unit who was a solicitor, and had done some good court martials. When I asked for him to represent me the commandant nearly went bloody mad – "You can't have him! You're not holding up this unit's work, just to suit yourself. You're not running this show." And then he reverted to pleading with me that in my best interests I should have an officer to defend me.

Eventually they parked a bloke on me, who worked on the defence that I couldn't get out of the charge – which I knew – and that my reaction of being pushed was one of a trained soldier – to react to violence in a violent way. In the event I was found guilty and I was sentenced to six months.

My troubles really started when I got to the detention barracks in Chorley

Immediately I came across a staff sergeant on the section, on the first morning I was there, who looked at the charge sheet, where it said "Striking a superior officer." I was the only prisoner in the jail on such a charge. The first thing this bloke said, on reading it was "Six months? You should have got two years!" I thought: I'm well away with this bloke. I immediately dived across the room, and I was grabbed and held. I made a bit of an altercation – but that did what I wanted it to do – it got me in front of the commandant of the detention barracks. I explained the situation to him. I said "The two of us can't live in the same room. You either put me on a different section or you take him away." He wasn't a stupid man. In the event they put him on another section, and they noted, not for the first time, that I was a tailor, and would I like to work in the tailor's shop? That got me through my detention in relative comfort. Nevertheless, it was no picnic, particularly the trauma of reception, and search, and bathing and all the incidents that occurred.

I was in detention just after the Chatham manslaughter charge, in which two Staff Sergeants were sentenced for manslaughter and dismissed, for beating up a prisoner who had TB and killing him in the process

As a result there'd been a big switch round in staff and a new system of so-called "checks". One of the inmates at Chorley was a bloke who had escaped from Poland at the beginning of the war, and when he arrived here in England he volunteered. He was in his middle-forties. He was one those people who had two left legs and two left arms – he just could not do the drill. He was a constant butt in his unit. He was in the Pioneer Corps. He was an intelligent, educated man. He could speak English. After a while life became impossible for him – he was the butt for everybody's whatsisname. Not only that, physically he couldn't do the damn thing, and he's suffering. So he deserted from the Pioneer Corps and he got caught and court martialled. He finished up in detention.

Course, here he was at an even bigger disadvantage. Here there was no escaping at all. They tried to persevere, but there was no way they were going to teach him to slope arms, keep in step, or whatever. He just couldn't do it. So they gave him a job in the industrial part, which was to clean the baking tins and billy cans that had come back from field kitchens. That means they were black, and I mean black – thick and crusted with burnt fat. You had to bring them up with brick dust. That was the only cleaning material that existed in those places. He was in a hut kind of place, which was near where I was working in the tailoring workshop. This was a flat-roofed outbuilding, apart from the main building. It was an old mill, this place at Chorley.

On the other side of this outbuilding was a tower with a couple of hosepipes hanging down. Instead of ascertaining whether these hoses were fixed at the top, or just hanging to dry, he decided to escape one day. He climbed on the roof, grabbed the hosepipe and fell to the ground. The hosepipe was simply hanging, drying. Before anyone had any chance to see if he's broken any bones – it wasn't any great height – they pounced on him. They beat the shit out of him.

They were beating him all the way to the cells

An old boy who'd been on the sewing machine with me, who'd landed in the chokey for something he'd done, and another young bloke, were either side of the Pole's cell. They heard him being beaten up, crying and screaming, and this was the time, as I said, just after the Chatham manslaughter charge. There was a new system in operation that meant that the inmates of the detention camp were paraded – I think it was every Friday morning – one day a week. A Major or field officer would come from a surrounding command.

You're all paraded there and a statement would be read out, something like "Anybody wishing to complain, double out now!" Well, no one ever did! Who was going to stick their necks out and complain! But on this occasion this old boy and the young feller were so outraged by the way this bloke got beaten up that they decided to complain. They doubled out and complained.

Of course, normal thing – "There will be a court of inquiry, blah, blah, blah." Unknown to them, though, the authorities got hold of the Pole and told him "Don't make too much fuss and you'll get your ticket after the court of inquiry." By this time he was medically and mentally unacceptable to the army. When the court of inquiry came, he said no one hit him! And these two poor sods were on a charge of making false accusations.

This is the nature of the organisation. This is the system that keeps everybody in order. There is no way in which you can defeat them without drawing to yourself the direst consequences.

18 When a lot of guys were abroad the other guys were kipping up with their wives

Fusilier That's something that's no said much about the war, yet I think it's something most people know about. I done it myself. I slept with a couple of women when their men were abroad. They were getting their money every week, buying the booze with it – all that stuff. There was no really a great deal of loyalty. The other side of the coin was when I was in India guys I knew used to get "Dear John" letters. Some of the guys took it pretty bad and shot themselves.

Woman Warworker Me and my mates, we got on this penfriend thing to lads in the forces, and we put "Miss" instead of "Mrs". We got loads of letters back. And then they'd write "I'm going home on leave, looking ever so forward to meeting you" and we'd write back and say we'd moved and forget to give the new address. It was just a joke for us.

Flight Sergeant Girls in uniform were often referred to as "Officers' Groundsheets". In our case I don't think airforce men went out with Waafs particularly. In fact, just the opposite. They tended to shy away from women in their own uniform and go for women in the Wrens, Land Army . . . Most stations I went to you usually got a lecture from the MO about

"There was the attitude about girls in uniform, that they were easy, but they weren't any different from other girls."

V.D. The day I got my wing and my three stripes I was ushered one afternoon into a cinema to see a horrifying film on V.D. God! There were people passing out right, left and centre. It was a camp cinema. The idea was, in some people's eyes, aircrew had a certain glamour – you found it easier to get girls because you had more money than other people, so now that you were a sergeant and you had a wing, this is what you could get unless you were careful.

Waaf There was the attitude about girls in uniform, that they were easy, but really speaking, they weren't. They weren't any different from other girls. The girls I knew were a real good lot. You always had a real good friend. At Torquay we had the Dutch airmen. They were ever so polite. I'll tell you what though, our blokes in uniform . . . Once I smacked one round the chops. This was at Gloucester, at a dance. Me and my mate, we used to put our civvies underneath our uniform, and then we'd go in the cloakroom and take our uniform off. I'm dancing with this airman, he was a sergeant, and he didn't know I was a Waaf.

"You're a nice girl" he said "Can I see you home tonight? 'Cos," he said "these Waafs" he said "they're nothing like you girls in civvies." We're dancing around the floor and I'm kidding him on. "Oh yeah?" I says "Don't you think girls in uniform aren't nice?" "What? They're the lowest of the low." "Oh? Do you think so. You know what you can do, don't you!" I gave him one round the chops and I walked off the floor and left him. He came over and apologised, but I didn't half give him a mouthful.

When we was at Torquay we used to go out to Newton Abbot, to the Yankee dances. We used to have a real good time with them, and they always used to bring us straight back. They always treated us with respect. A lot of that feeling against them was just jealousy.

Somerset Farmer They brought a lot of white Americans round Shepton Mallet and Evercreech. There was lot of – what you call it? Cohibition? Cohabitation? – that some of the authorities and some of the people were a little bit disturbed, 'cos most of the women were married and their husbands was fighting for the country. So they took the white Americans away and brought a lot of black Yanks around. They thought that would stop it. Well, these women that were cohabiting with the white Americans, they started cohabiting with black ones. Not one of those fell pregnant until within three weeks of their going abroad. When they men went abroad they didn't know they were pregnant, but they knew they were pregnant a week after they were gone! And none of them could claim off of them, you see, 'cos they were gone. And one of them was a —————'s wife.

The thing that struck me as a young lad was the change in morality

Teeside Lad Around Middlesbrough you were poor but you were honest. You try take a ha'penny out of mother's purse and she'd chop your fingers off. During war, when husbands started going away, everything went. Fourteen year old lasses, 15 year old lasses used to have Polish seamen, Yanks,

Canadians – the bloody lot. They'd cock their legs up for a couple of bloody coppers.

I had a mate and I used to spend a lot of time at their house. He got a sister about 17 year old, and his mother was a barmaid. Her husband was in Royal Engineers and he was in reserve. As soon as war come he were called up, and she were having it off. They had an aunty living with them, and this aunty was married to a feller called ——— ———. He was what they called a Dems gunner on merchant ships. Dems was Defence Equipment of Merchant Ships. They used to have a big 10,000 ton tanker and they used to shove one of these fellers on board with a little bloody Lewis gun up front.

This feller had done about five convoys to Russia. One time when he come back he'd bought all these Chinese dresses – silk, high collars and split down side, and he'd bought a great big astrakhan coat. He fetches them all and lays them before his wife, but she couldn't care less because she was cocking her leg round at ——— Hotel. She was kipping with Americans, Canadians, the lot. She was living the life of luxury – all the clothes she wanted, all the cigarettes she wanted. Lays it all before her. "I just can't be bothered tonight because I'm working." Poor cunt, he's come back from Russia, touch of DTs and God knows what, and he's sat with all this fucking gear. I would only be about 13 and sat commiserating with him, smoking his cigarettes. What can you do? He was pouring his bloody heart out and I was only a young lad. He only got about two days and back he goes to sea.

---

19 When we were getting near France and I realised this was it I was like a jelly-nerves. I wasn't no hero

---

London Lad I had a marvellous experience at work. I had supposed to have studied French at school and I had a vague knowledge of it, about enough to say "Hallo" to somebody. I worked as an apprentice making radios. I got one of these radios going and they announced the D day landings – in French. It hadn't been announced in English. The bloke I was working for had been a pilot in the Spanish Civil War, on the Republican side, and I called him down. It kept giving out these reports, and he could understand. I ran out into the street and told everyone the army had landed and nobody would believe me. I was really upset as I knew the armies had landed.

Royal Engineer I was in the first wave on D day. It was supposed to be half past six in the morning, but we was late again! The British Army was late again! Eight o'clock we got there. We went from Gosport. We was kept up there for six weeks in the "cages" – a big white camp, all under canvas. You couldn't get outside the perimeter wire. They had guards on it – Redcaps and dogs. We had all our last minute secret training in there, but no-one knew when it was going to be. They was all over England, these camps. You kept doing the same thing over and over again.

Fusilier During pre-D day landing exercises at places like Inverary and Rothesay guys were throwing their weapons overboard. This was no just a matter of them larking around. The reason for throwing phosphorous grenades and dumping their bullets and bombs overboard was that they just didnae want to know. They didn't want to get their faces burned or a bullet through the bloody head.

Royal Engineer Once a week we had to all put on our battle order. We had special assault jackets, different to the army uniform. They put us on lorries and took us to Gosport harbour. We embarked on tank landing craft and they took you out into the Channel. Maybe four hours. The next week you thought: Hallo? What's going on here? We were away, so we thought. But they brought you back – back to the routine. We didn't know when we were going out whether it was training or for real.

Of course, the last time they took us out I thought to myself: We're out here a fucking long time. And the blokes are saying "What the hell's going on today? We want to get back." Then the Captain who's driving the boat came round and gave you the word – that this was the real thing. The old padre came at us, and you're going "Cor, fucking hell! I wish I'd known this! They wouldn't have got me out!"

Fusilier At the height of the Normandy landings almost every police station and detention camp in Britain was jam-packed full. In Glasgow alone, at places like Blythswood Police Station, deserters were sitting twelve in a cell. Maryhill Barracks was like the Black Hole of Calcutta – Edinburgh Castle likewise, and the story was repeated up and down the country.

Royal Engineer On the boat you was all split up into your little groups. They split everybody up into small groups so that in case of casualties – in case a whole lot got wiped out – you still had a unit. There was only me and mate of mine – us two engineers on that one boat. Then we had an anti-aircraft gun, bren carrier, few infantrymen, few ambulance men – all mixed, so that whoever got there, you had something of each.

You had your map reference when you landed, where to go. If you were interested. Course, some went that way, and some went the other way! But where could you desert to?

You took a chance whatever way you went. You didn't know what you was going in to. When we were getting near France and I realised this was it I was like a jelly – nerves. I wasn't no hero. I don't think nobody was. I was a coward. I admit that. It's a sensation you can't explain. It's a gradual process. It's like indoctrination. After a couple of days you're getting used to it. Someone's slinging shells at you and it goes Bang! Bang! – and you're diving in holes. It becomes a matter of – like a rabbit – you come out to feed and do something, and every time the noise goes – you're down the hole. I was the fastest one of the lot!

Where we landed was only a narrow beach, about fifty yards wide, and the tide had started to go out. We were supposed to have got in on a full tide, but as we were late it was on its way out. We was about 50 yards out, but the Captain of the boat said "You'll be alright, I'll run you right up to the beach", which he did. They were all doing that – banging them right up

"I wasn't no hero. I don't think nobody was."

onto the beach. I hung on the barrel of the anti-aircraft gun, so I wouldn't get my arse wet. I wasn't going in the water for no fucker. When you landed you had all your colours – gold, red – and your boats went for that. We were getting shells. The Beachmasters landed first – blokes on the beach with flags, waving them in. They were fucking heros – all them blokes.

Everbody was on the beach. It was jammed up. They had a casualty clearing station up one end, dug in some cliffs. They was taking the casualties in there. There was a little stone wall – a parapet wall along the front and we was behind that, crouching. All of us. No fucker would move. They was all piling up behind there. It was Bénouville beach we'd landed on, though no one tried to tell you what your objective was. Ours was Bénouville Bridge. We had to meet up with the 6th Airborne who'd landed in front of us and captured the bridge. But we didn't know whether they'd captured it or not! No one knew how to get to where they were supposed to go. You'd say "Where you going mate?" You walked, run or got a lift up there. We were like a load of kids on an outing, everyone's wandering around.

As soon as they realised the first attack had gone in and it was serious they started slinging a few shells back. It was every man for himself. There was a bit of an opening where the road came down to the beach and they was all making for that. And the first thing I see, laying in the middle of the road was a green beret and a blown up bike. All smoking. Bits of rag. He got a direct hit with a mortar, this commando. They landed with them folding bikes. That was the first one I saw. I thought: Oh no. I didn't want to know much, so me and my mate Tosh thought: Let's fuck off and get out of it. We shot up the road into a churchyard. We sat there for a couple of hours. Had a fag. Thought: Fuck it, what are we going to do now? We gradually worked our way up. As we were going up they came over and dropped another load of airborne troops. The 6th Airborne went in first – the old Flying Horse Pegasus. They called it Pegasus Bridge afterwards.

I was in the forward area all the time. It was a three mile area, which wasn't very nice because you was getting the short distance shells, and you went up with the infantry

Some of the infantry wouldn't move without us, and we wouldn't move without the infantry – that's how you used to argue! It's unbelievable. If they had to go out on a night patrol and they came up against a minefield they'd send back for us. "Fuck you", we'd say, "We're not going up there to get shot" – and you're standing there arguing. That's how the army was running. The officers would sort it out. A sapper in the RE's was equal to an infantry lieutenant. When the poor infantry used to quake in their shoes at a lieutenant, we used to tell them to fuck off.

After a couple of days at D day the next wave landed and they went up to take over from our division, but they ran into a counter-attack, and got knocked back. Our division, our infantry had to hold on where they were. It was six weeks before we got a break, we got a rest. First thing we had to do was lay 2000 mines, right across our own area. This was all night work. Couldn't do it by day – they'd see you. You had no time that was your own. You lived from day to night, day to night. Working and sleeping, working and sleeping. You got so it was your last day. Do what you could today – it didn't matter about tomorrow. Anything could happen.

You see some weird things in war. Once you get involved in a war, I don't care who you are, if you're up in the forward area, where there's any action, I say every man turned into an animal. The conversion was gradual. From the time you were there you started living like an animal. You got involved in casualties, in dead bodies, and living in holes in the ground, in old bombed houses. You gradually changed. Didn't matter how timid or what sort of person you was, you became an animal. You didn't notice it. When you first arrived after D day and you see a couple of bodies blown to bits, it turns you up, and you're looking to see if you could do anything. Three weeks, a month later, they're still lying there. You just walk past them.

None of our lot deserted in Germany, but I think there was quite a few infantry blokes who went on the run. They'd had enough of it. Once they got in a town I suppose they thought: Why go any further? They'd had enough.

Once I got 14 days leave from the Dortmund-Ems Canal. We was putting a bridge across there, to get our infantry across. There was a little village and the road ran straight down to the canal. We put a folding boatbridge across. We were sleeping in a farm, a mile back down the road, and they started shelling the boatbridge. They'd wait until you've finished it, then they'd blow a big hole in it. This Corporal, when I got back he said to me "You've got 14 days leave, starting tomorrow." It was a rota system. Only one of you went, and it had come round to me. And then he says "They've blown one of our boats out the river – come on, we've got to go back up there." I said "You go and get stuffed. I'd rather be shot than go back there, Bill." He was a nice bloke. "You and no-one else is going to get me back there." "I'll have to report you." "You'll have to shoot me. I'm not going back there."

I got back to England by train and boat. The driver took me to the nearest town with the water cart the following morning and I got a train from there, I still went back to my unit though. I must have been mad. I must have been potty. Mind, I was five days adrift. I let them keep going forward. Trouble was, they stopped and I caught up with them. I suppose the fact that I came back was part of the British Army inborn discipline – 'cos you'd do it in England. They'd say "Fourteen days. Report back so and so a day, 1200 hours." You automatically think "I've got to be there at 12."

They were very strict on fraternisation with Germans. Very strict

I never heard of anyone getting caught for going out with a

German girl. They were too crafty to get caught. It was as much to do with the German population, as anybody, because they didn't want to know you, even if you wanted to fraternise.

It wasn't all Germans you could get off. You got Dutch – all kinds. One place in Holland the locals had to go from one town to another place to collect their potato rations. I was working on the road there, and you'd see these girls carrying a half hundredweight in a sack, walking along the road. Blokes would give them a bar of chocolate and they'd hop over the hedge and have a jump for a bar of chocolate. It was survival. Couldn't blame 'em for doing it.

With kids, you couldn't really stop fraternisation. They couldn't understand, could they? If they spoke to you – what could you do? Couldn't just kick 'em up the arse. But I don't mind the Germans myself. I found them better than anybody, because they were the nearest to English people that I've seen – the English breed. They had exactly the same habits, in all ways. The same attitudes. I mean, you could offer them a fag and they'd tell you to stick it up your arse. Some of the others, they'd come crawling up for fags.

At first they was allowed to bring back anything, but they had to put a stop to it

Some of these people were bringing back furniture. I seen one bloke when I came on that leave, he had a small baby piano on his back, strapped to his back, coming down the gangplank. A little German miniature piano. I didn't have nothing – No – Yes I did – a kind of horse blanket I'd been using to sit on. It was black one side and leopard skin the other. I've still got it, in fact. But it got so bad they had to stop it. They were looting everything. It was mainly the blokes behind the line – artillery and corps troops. They was packing it up in packing cases, labelling it and sending it home. But they had to put a stop to it.

The V2's, they were dreadful bombs. That was when the Nazis were on their last knockings

London Lad They were dreadful bombs.[1] You never knew

when they were coming. There was no warning. There was not **135**
even an air raid siren. They just came down and exploded.

London Woman Them flying bombs were shockers. They were
the V1s. You'd see what looked like a little flame, and it'd go
sailing over and you'd feel quite safe – safe whilst it was moving
and making a noise. There was no harm at all. But the minute it
stopped! Pandemonium would break out.

Company Sergeant-Major I was on leave from Africa and
every time one of those fly bombs used to come over I used to
get frightened stiff. They used to go off every time you sat down
to a meal. The siren would go and as soon as it went my
stomach turned over and over. When the siren packed up and
you came back to have a bit to eat, you didn't want anything.
Everything went to my stomach.

One of the finest sights I saw when I did come home was a
thousand bomber raid. We were going over to friends that
evening. A fly bomb had dropped near Prince Regent Lane and
I wanted to see it. All I saw was people picking up their beds
and walking along the streets. They were filthy. I hadn't seen
things like that. On the way there we were going along the
Sewer Bank and there was this tremendous noise and you
looked up and the sky – you couldn't see it for planes. It was a
wonderful feeling that was.

Airman, RAF Regiment In 1945 we were in Holland guarding
airfields. It was terrible because the Germans had blown up the
dykes and everything was flooded. I used to see the planes
going over in Holland. It must have been hell in those German
cities. They were bombed by the British during the night and by
the Americans by day. I could imagine what it was like. It must
have been terrible.

---

[1] The V2s, unlike the V1s, travelled so quickly that they were rarely heard,
nor was there time for an alert.

The maximum sentence for disaffection of the forces under regulation 1AA was 15 years. We didn't know what to expect

Anarchist During the war the anarchist movement was pretty well a closed shop, as of course it had to be. There was the overt activity – the open public activity, and there was the underground stuff going on. There was the whole business of having to protect deserters and people on the run. There had to be security.

The overt activity of the Freedom Group[1] was things like public speaking at Hyde Park and publishing *War Commentary*, which had an uninterrupted run through the war. We printed about 3000 per edition, which was a modest print order. We got our allocation of newsprint and paper because it was a publishing house that had been established before the war. We sold the bulk of what we printed. We had good sales, here in London and a very, very good and active group in Glasgow. The ILP[2] was very strong there too. It was still the time when people talked about the "Red Clyde", and that whole period of the strong ILP. Besides us and the ILP, the SPGB[3] was the other political group that was totally opposed to the war.

I had a little studio then, in Camden Town, in Camden Street, which was a very nice secluded place behind a church, with an alleyway leading to it. We had a problem of where to put a rather special deserter who had just come out of the army to join us. He was a chap called John Olday. He was of German origins who'd been in the German anarchist movement and had come over here just before the war. He'd been drafted into the Pioneer Corps and was in it for a couple of years. He was a cartoonist and had been sending his cartoons to *War Commentary* – very, very sharp, acid and funny cartoons.

The time came when he decided he could no longer stand it and wanted to pull out. So we had to give him some place to live

"We had good sales, here in London and a very good and active group in Glasgow."

and this studio of mine was just right. He came and lived with me in that studio for quite a few months. He established a network of communication with dissident soldiers. He started a regular monthly newsletter – soldiers' newsletter – which was duplicated. He sent this out to a list of about 200 soldiers. His special knowledge of the army gave him the opportunity to talk in their terms and establish a rapport with soldiers which us conchies didn't have.

Besides publishing *War Commentary* we also turned out an unending stream of little penny pamphlets and sixpenny booklets. In the autumn of 1944, when the State decided to attack us, I was off on a bookselling tour. We'd drawn up a big itinerary, starting from London up to Bristol, up the west country, up to Glasgow, across to Edinburgh, and right the way down, covering every major town. It was an absolute joy. I sold £500 worth of literature in six weeks! I was sending orders down and they were having to get some things back on the press because they were right out.

It was at this time that John Olday got picked up. He kept mum for a long time – wouldn't say who he was, but eventually they found out and it coincided with some things we were saying in the paper that they were objecting to. They raided my studio and found all his stuff – the duplicating machine, and discovered that letters had been circulating among soldiers. As

". . . we also turned out an unending stream of little pamphlets and sixpenny booklets."

a result of this they raided Freedom Press and because I was on the bookselling tour they found my ration book and they said "What's this?" You could stay one night in a hotel without a ration book, so I'd left it behind for other people to pick up their rations. They also found in my studio a lovely great sheepskin coat which I'd bought from a soldier when I had been working on the land and had a motorbike.

As a result of them raiding my place and Freedom Press, as a consequence of picking up John Olday, the whole bloody balloon went up. By the time I came back to London I had to go into hiding. They'd nabbed three of the others. They'd picked up Vernon Richards, who was nominally the owner of Express Printers, the movement's printing press, and John Hewetson, who was a doctor, and he was nominally the owner of Freedom Press. The third was Marie-Louise, Vernon Richards' wife. A short while after I'd got back I was jumped on in a friend's flat. Someone had squealed that I was staying there.

So there were the four of us. John Olday was already in nick.

The maximum sentence for disaffection of the forces under regulation 1AA was 15 years. We didn't know what to expect. The Disaffection Act of 1934 had laid down two years maximum but the wartime regulations upped that to 15 years. A few months before, us four Trotskyists had been done for inciting a strike in Newcastle – the famous Apprentices' Strike – and they'd got six months, I think, just for that. Our thing seemed to be getting a hell of a lot more attention. We were anticipating two. maybe three years.

When we were attacked the amount of support we got from all sorts of directions, including people like Orwell, was astonishing

They rallied around in an absolutely marvellous way. Freedom Press had an enormous amount of prestige at that time and a lot of affection going for it, and a lot of respect. It had grown out of the Spanish war, which was still not all that far behind, and so a lot of people rallied around. I'm never going to hear anything against old Herbert Read[4] on account of what he did at the time. He roped in all the bloody intellectuals, with his name behind us, and Ethel Mannin and old pacifists with prestige like Reginald Reynolds, and a few other people like that. And we got MPs on the Defence Committee – Michael Foot, Fenner Brockway. The left MPs joined up. Bevan joined us as patron of the Freedom Press Defence Committee, and people like Orwell wrote, and the whole thing began to thunder. We set up a defence fund and we raised £2000 in a very short time, with the result that we were able to buy the services of top-flight barristers.

We put it forward and it was accepted as a freedom of speech thing. This was Orwell's attitude. He made it perfectly clear he didn't agree with us about the war, but he was concerned with the freedom of speech issue. He spoke on our platforms, both before and afterwards. The Freedom Committee was kept going after the trial as a sort of alternative to the NCCL[5] which at the time was heavily CP[6] dominated.

When I was arrested the police found that I hadn't notified my last change of address on my Identity Card. I was charged on two counts, besides the Disaffection charge. One for not notifying my change of address and two, for being in possession of Government property – the army sheepskin coat I'd bought off this soldier. I was given a month on each count, just to keep me in while they were cooking up the main charges. I was in nick when the first hearings began in the magistrates' court for the general charges against Freedom Press.

When we finally got weighed off at the Old Bailey and got nine months each we were highly delighted! We'd been expecting a lot more. Marie-Louise was found not guilty on a technicality. As I had already done some time, because of the other offences, I was classed as a second-timer and I was sent to Wandsworth, which was a hell of a jail. After a week at Wandsworth I applied for a transfer to the Scrubs, where the others were, but instead they sent me to Maidstone, which was a lovely little nick.

I had no complaints at Maidstone at all. It was small, very pleasant and the sun was shining. It was mid-summer. They put me to work in the print-shop. Here was I, having been done for making propaganda to disaffect the forces, actually being taught how to print! It was marvellous! Unfortunately I was stupid enough to write out and say this in my letters and the Special Branch were of course reading them, so after a week in Maidstone I was hurriedly sent back to Wandsworth. I applied again for a transfer and eventually they did send me to the Scrubs. There we had a great time. Apart from the criminals in there, who were not a great lot, most of the chaps were deserters. There wasn't a hostile atmosphere in there. We set ourselves up very quickly to become a kind of advisory body, and Hewetson, as a doctor, always had his ear bent to various complaints. We became quite a nice little influence.

The trial happened at a time when the war was obviously coming to an end and the Allies were obviously winning. Had it happened in the atmosphere of 1940 it might have been quite a different story. But by 1945 people were pissed off by the war.

---

[1] The focal point of the wartime British anarchist movement.
[2] Independent Labour Party.
[3] Socialist Party of Great Britain.
[4] Herbert Read sullied his name amongst many anarchists when he accepted a knighthood for "Services to Literature" in 1953.
[5] National Council for Civil Liberties.
[6] Communist Party.

21 We all had visions of Socialism then

London Lad VE day was one of the most emotional days in my life. There were Union Jacks out and everyone was saying "We want the King!" Everyone was shouting for the King. Men and women. Mind you, they were shouting for Louis XVI a few weeks before they cut his head off. You can't go on the emotions of . . . People were so pent up. There was mass shagging in the streets . . . No sort of class distinction. I walked into a posh hotel and everyone was offering me drinks. Everybody. What amazed me was where they got the drink from! No one ever had it – at least, we didn't, because before this, pubs were closed. People had to walk miles to get a drink. A bloke would say to another bloke "I know a pub that's got some beer." The pub would be packed solid until they drank the beer out. So I don't know where they got the drink from.

Miner VE day they give you money to stop in. I was on nights when word came through – day's pay and home James, and don't spare the horses! Extra pint in pub! Extra ale!

West Country Girl On VE day they had bonfires on hilltops. They took weeks building up huge bonfires on all the hills – on Street Hill and on Wearyall Hill, between Street and Glastonbury, and all the hills around. As soon as VE day came they lit the bonfires one after the other. It was marvellous. Everyone went to the bonfire in their district.

West Country Boy From Ham Hill we could see all the other fires. A sailor at our fire actually threw himself in the middle of the bonfire and they had to haul him off. He was in flames. They had to roll him down the hill to put the flames out. He was drunk. That was Victory night.

2nd West Country Girl VE day in Winscombe was very dead. We were longing for something. We could have gone to Weston but there wasn't a late bus to come back. We really felt left out of things. You read about all these marvellous things going on in London – dancing in the streets.

East London Girl On VE day I watched my dad dance up and down the street. He was dead drunk, my dad was. He tap danced all up and down our street. My dad used to have cups for tap dancing. Everybody was out on the street, drunk. We watched from the window.

Liverpool Lass On VE night there was a gang of us got together. We were still working on the railway, this gang. We were on 2 to 11 shift, my mate and I. We got that much drink, we walked up from Central Station and the next thing we remembered doing was sitting in Abercromby Square Gardens about four in the morning – singing. I don't think anyone slept. Everyone went mad those two days.

Boy Soldier We were stationed at Catterick and a gang of us went to Middlesbrough. There was a lad called ————— from Newcastle, and he took a box of hand-grenades and a bloody great box of flares. In Middlesbrough he was throwing these hand-grenades in park. We finished up in Acland Road. We came across a pile of road chippings and bloody barrels of tar. How we did it I don't know, but we got about three of these barrels stacked one on top of the other and set fire to bottom one, and we were all dancing around them. VE day. Get on there!

During the 1945 election I was stationed at Hunstanton in Norfolk

Leeds Man The government had agreed that soldiers could take part in the elections but not dressed in army uniform. There was nothing in Hunstanton. I thought "I'll have to do something here." I went to the local Co-op and I asked to see the manager. I asked him "Are you a member of the Labour Party?" "It so happens I am. Why?" "Where is the Labour Party?" "We haven't got any Labour Party." "How about forming one?" "It's a good idea. Look," he says, "go down the railway station." The railway station clerk was the station master, signals, porter, clerk, luggage man – he was the whole lot. And he was delighted. I said "Do you know anybody?" "Yes" he said. "I know a bus driver and his wife who are Labour." And there was also the War Agricultural Officer, the man who looked after the farms. I went to see this lad and I've been friends with him ever since.

"What are we going to do?" he says. "We're going to form a Labour Party." We called a meeting. We had about a dozen people. None of them were public speakers. I was the only one who could stand up in public. The bus driver had a belly as big as Fatty Arbuckle's, and he lent me a pair of trousers and a sports coat. I used to go to this Agricultural Officer's house, change into the trousers, sew them up the back to make them fit (he always had to have them back the same night, so I always had to sew them up everytime), and I'd go travelling round villages making public speeches. Our candidate was a Major Wise. The headquarters were in King's Lynn – but we won the blessed seat. We won it! Everybody was shattered that we won it.

London Lad At the time of the General Election the *Daily Mirror* invited youth to write an article and I wrote an article saying how I thought Labour would deal with it. I was really proud of seeing me name in print. I showed it to everybody. In those days I thought Labour was the be-all and end-all of everything. We all had visions of socialism then.

Conscript I was on a boat going to India when the election results came over the tannoy. When we heard Labour had won – now this is a true story – all the soldiers on this troopship, thousands of them – got up and sang the *Red Flag*. The officers couldn't stop it. They didn't try.

When the Smithfield porters were out on strike we were detailed to go and work in Smithfield market[1]

Paratrooper We were supposed to blackleg. We had three ton Bedfords, down at Shorncliffe, I was driving them at the time. They said "Right, make your way to Smithfield." I was in the second lorry and my mate was driving the first one. There was about 20 to 30 blokes in each lorry and there were four lorries. I said to my mate "Do you know your way to Smithfield?" "I haven't a fucking clue" he said. "Follow me" I said, "I'll take you to Smithfield."

Know where we finished up? Hastings. We had a great time,

mucking about on the beach. I wasn't going to lead those lorries to Smithfield. All the drivers were put on a charge. They couldn't say nothing to the soldiers. I took the responsibility. I said "Look, I thought I knew the way to London, but I must have took the wrong turning." They couldn't do nothing about it, but we was confined to camp for five days. I wasn't going to go up there and do that – break the strike. All the lads were in agreement. We all had a day out, down by the seaside.

Driver, North African Campaign I believe, in fact I'm bloody sure, that when the war was over and the Labour government got in – not that I've got any time for them now – I believe it was because of the fact that at the time of the war the Tories were in power. They felt the Tories were to blame for not seeing the wood for the trees and arming up earlier so that we would be in a position to say to Hitler "Pack it up."

London Lad A lot of people knew unconsciously that Churchill would be a great war leader because he was such an aggressive bastard. Years and years after the war, when Churchill died, they tried to set up a memorial fund for him, and they even had the temerity to put it to trade union branches. The war was in 1939. There were men who were adolescents in 1912 when he did the Tonypandy killings. Thirteen years before 1939 Churchill had been very, very active in the '26 strike. The extent of people voting for Labour proved that a lot of them had no time for him, and the Tories and *The Times* and the *Telegraph* and the *Observer* couldn't understand it. They were saying "How can they do this to our great war leader?"

Demobbed? I finished up in Jerusalem! Helping out the Palestine police

Royal Engineer That's the part that got me – I was called up for four years fighting against the Germans to protect the Jews. When it ended, they flew us, as an emergency, from Germany to Brussels airport, Brussels airport to Cairo, to fight the Jews! They were killing British Palestine police.

What happened was, they changed the division over into a Flying Squad effort, being the Light Infantry Division. It was snowing when we left. We was at Knokke first – Knokke,

Belgium – and then we went to Brussels. They bunged us all on planes and we was away. Landed at Cairo West airport, with all our gear. They put us on lorries and it took three days to cross the Sinai desert, and we had no issue. We were still in khaki and sweating like pigs. Lips coming out like balloons. Three days.

When we got there, there was another balls-up. First job we had to do was building nissen huts to put all the extra infantry in, that was landing. I thought to myself: I don't know – I've been chasing Germans for the last four years to protect the Jews and now we're chasing the Jews to protect ourselves. We was all a bit perplexed, but no one was really interested, though, in what was happening. After that sort of time you just followed orders. You woke up in the morning, someone says such and such and you say "Yeah, alright."

We were getting up at five in the morning and stringing barbed wire all round the streets and capturing all the Jews and taking them to the detention camp. Being the RE's we was also on explosives. It took us three months – this is laughable – it took us three months to put barbed wire round the King David Hotel in Jerusalem. We hung it around the roofs, we hung it around the doors, we hung it everywhere. Three solid months – rolls of barbed wire. One morning two milkmen walk in the door, with their white coats and a churn of explosives, stood it in the door and blew the fucking lot up.

I was at Aldershot when I got demobbed

Paratrooper When the war in Europe finished this officer came round and said "You'll still have your chance. We're still fighting out in Japan." I said "Bleeding good luck to you. I don't want to go to bloody Japan." But then the war in Japan packed up and we got sent to Aldershot.

We was getting called in one by one and getting told "If you like to stay on we'll make you a sergeant." I said "No mate, you stick your army, I've had enough." We went down to Guildford to get our demob suit. You was all the same – Majors, Colonels, Captains – you was all waiting in the same place. All together. There was this Captain, he still had his tunic on so you could see his pips, and there was this little trilby hat, all alone on a shelf. I was making for it, and he came round the other way, but I got there first. He said "Oh, damn and blast!" and I said "And damn and blast you!"

I had the old pin stripe suit. You could keep your great-coat, respirator case and socks. I remember walking down the turning, where I lived with my mother-in-law, down in Stepney, carrying all me civvie gear in a big cardboard box. That was me – my soldiering days were over.

I was in one of the units that was training for the final assault on Japan

Fusilier It was the Black Watch. We're paratroopers, we're an airborne unit, and we were training in the jungle to maybe land in a city! When we found out this was what we were training for we were sweating blood!

When the war finished, I remember that as clear as day. I heard the noise coming all coming through the different parts. It was like as if somebody had lifted a ton weight. You didn't realise it was there – you'd become so accustomed to it. But suddenly it wasn't there and you say "I'm going to live now! I'm no going to die! I'm going to live!" And your outlook was completely different.

When the war was finished and we were still in the jungle they came around, a day or two after we'd heard the news. looking for volunteers to jump into prisoner of war camps, to bring in medical supplies and food – to let the lads see that the war was over and that they were thinking about them. But a lot of us knew that the Japanese were still fighting in places like that, and we didnae want to do it. A mate of mine who was a corporal comes up to me and says "Morry, if you want to live, get the hell out of it. They're coming looking for volunteers to jump into these different prisoner of war camps." And you couldnae find a man in the place! Everybody had disappeared. Nobody wanted to die after the war was finished.

I was medically examined for repatriation. It was discovered that because of a serious illness, connected to heat exhaustion I'd suffered, that my eyes had been affected. I was downgraded to B1 or B4, but I was warned that my demob would be more straightforward if I'd agree to being classed as A1. Lower grades, apparently, had to go through two courses of remedial treatment, which was intended to upgrade the disabled soldier before demob. Like others – not unnaturally – I chose to be upgraded to A1, in order to speed up my journey home and out of the forces. Later I learned that had I remained B4 I'd have been entitled to a war pension, and it makes me wonder how many blokes got this treatment to save the authorities money.

Prior to repatriation we were sent to special education classes which took the form of brainwashing. They were trying to prepare us for our homecoming. They were telling us we shouldn't be resentful when we found that our people back home just weren't interested in the war, or who had won it, or what you'd done, or where you'd been. They were too busy getting on with normal everyday living.

When I did get home, and I came off the train at Central Station and went to Hope Street to get myself a bus – loaded up with kitbags and God knows what, piled on top of my shoulders – despite the fact that I had been demobbed, had a demob suit and all the rest of it – I just couldnae get a bloody bus! Everybody jumped in and passed me to get on the bus. I was so angry about the situation that I walked the whole bloody road home rather than suffer the indignity of having to fight to get onto the bus. Nobody cared an arse about the homecoming soldier, or the veteran and his medals. Maybe that was to the good. People were totally disinterested. The show was over.

---

[1] On 8 April 1946, six hundred Smithfield workers came out on strike. On April 15 the Labour government sent troops in to break the strike. As a result 3000 meat porters struck work in sympathy.

22

When I came out the airforce I went up the Labour. I said "Can I have a job please?"

Scunthorpe Man I was demobbed June, 1946. I'd been in nearly seven years. They did offer for me to stay on but it was straight away "No." I wanted to be out, although, later on, you wonder whether you should have stayed on, for the security, and by then you were just starting to enjoy the life, more or less. You'd got used to it. When I came out ———— was a year old and there was no money in baking. Before the war I was apprenticed at the bakery. I didn't want to go to the steel works, but it was the biggest paid job that counted at that time, and you could get a bit of overtime up there. So that was it. I went there.

Waaf When I came out the airforce I went up the Labour. I said "Can I have a job please?" She said "What've you been doing?" I said "I've been doing post-office work" She said "You're not in the airforce now," She said "You're out, and I've only got one job here, and that's on the calculating punching machine." I said "What?" She said "At Holborn, in the Customs and Excise." I went there for a fortnight. It drove me mad. I had to work there otherwise they'd have cut me off. I'd have got no labour money. I was sitting down at a desk all day, not talking to anyone, so I chucked it in and I got a job up the Odeon, Barking Road. I was getting £2 a week.

Royal Engineer When I came out the army I didn't know where my wife and sister-in-law were living because they'd been moved a couple of times. Where they'd been staying was blasted by a V2. I eventually found that they were living in a requisitioned house in Woodford – Chigwell Road. I lived there for a while and started work in the building trade, but the bloke who owned the house wanted it back. He was a dentist and said he wanted it for his own living accommodation. When I went to the Housing Department at Woodford they said "We don't want your type here – you came from Stratford. You'll have to go back there."

I don't think anyone knew about the squatters until they were in

Scunthorpe Resident One family started putting furniture in, and then quite a few followed, before it got in the press. Once it was known it went all over the country, in the south. It was an army camp place. The nissen huts were still there. It had been a searchlight unit that had been there. They were all local folk, all from the town. One chap came out of there and lived next door to us at Newlands. He'd been in the navy.

For about a year or two after the war there were squatters in different parts of the town – anywhere where there were empty camps. It wasn't politically motivated.[1] It was just people coming back – some were living in with people, and perhaps with a child. This sort of thing. The idea of squatting just caught on. Even where the civil aerodrome was – it had been a big bomber base – you could see, going on your way to Grimsby – the washing hanging out. They were still squatting there long, long after the others had got cleared out of different places.

Before the war finished, anyone who was in the services and belonging to this area could put their name down on the council list. We got a place – a prefab – straight away on account of having the baby and TB in the house and over-crowded. When the housing position got better the folk who were squatting were moved out. Scunthorpe housing were soon on top of the situation.

Paratrooper I'd been away four years and I was sitting indoors. Boiling hot day and the old lady said to me "Why don't you go out ?" None of me mates was at home. I said "Alright, I'll go out for a walk round." As I goes out, I gets into the Heathway and I bumps into a bloke. He said "You been down the firm yet? They've got some money for you." "Eh? What?" "Yeah," he said, "you know they paid out for holiday bonus (they used to give you £5 at the start of the summer holiday), well, they've been putting that away for the blokes in the forces." I went down and saw about it.

I went down on the Friday. I walked into the firm, and honest, I was glad to get out! The noise was deafening! After being away all that time I'd forgotten just how bad it was. There was all the banging and clattering. I thought: Sod this. I went up the office and I picked up fifteen quid. I saw some of the lads. "Look at him. The old Red Berry on." "Yeah" I said, "it's a load of shit". All the time you was in the forces Briggs kept you on the books, and when I came out the forces, things was bad.

There was a fuel crisis. There was no coal. You had to queue up for coal. I still had my greatcoat, and I was glad of it. I daresay that if I'd looked round I might have found something different, but at that time I was married and the first child was on the way. I went back to the same job at Briggs I was doing before I got called up. I was there three days and it didn't seem as if I'd been away. I thought: I don't know, after all what's happened you come back and you're doing exactly the same job! After a couple of days it seemed that all that four years was nothing.

Jamaican Airgunner At the end of the war we had so much spare time on our hands that we was getting bored in camp. Quite a few, like myself, applied to Bennet College in Bristol to take a correspondence course. I apply and got everything through. Then I was posted to Burtonwood and I continued with the course. I had the intention that when I came out the airforce I would continue with it. But when I came out I find that you got to work.

I got a job near Rochdale – Castleton Moor. In those days the fog was very bad. As soon as, say, three o'clock come, down come the fog. It was very thick and two or three nights I had to walk it from Castleton Moor. I was living by Denmark Road, here in Manchester. I had an attic room I rented. When I had to walk it I didn't reach home until half past one, for the buses, they used to come from Rochdale and they used to turn round at what they call The Boundary, between Manchester and Rochdale. They didn't go further than that because the fog was so bad. Everybody had to get off the bus and walk it. It was just impossible – I couldn't work and study, so I had to give up my studying. When the war came to an end I was thinking of staying just until I could finish the course I was doing, get the degree out of it, and go back to Jamaica. But it didn't work out that way. I've never been back to Jamaica since I left.

---

[1] This was not necessarily the case by the time the squatting reached London.

---

23 Let's face it – who cared about the Jews?

West Country Girl I was at the Odeon in Weston and they had pictures of the extermination camps on the news. I've never seen anything like it. You'd heard, but you couldn't believe that people . . . Until you saw . . . It was the most terrible thing.

Glasgow Girl It was when we first saw the photos of the concentration camps that I realised, and I think most people realised that they were fighting for something, although maybe we didn't know it. As far as I was concerned I could have been fighting for the Russians, for the Germans, for the British or whoever it was. It was just nonsense. But that identified it, at least, and although no-one was aware of that at the beginning of the war, I think possibly it salved our consciences away for continuing to fight instead of saying "No, I'm not going to fight."

Anarchist I must admit that when I realised the full extent of the horror of what the Nazis were doing I was really shaken. It was very easy if you were against the war to believe that everything was propaganda. In the First World War a lot of propaganda had been invented – stories of Germans walking through Belgium with babies on their bayonets, and all this sort of thing. After, it had been exposed for what it was – lies, so we were ready to be suspicious about anything. I think it was bloody useful for the British that at the end of the war that the Nazis actually showed themselves to be the absolute bastards they were, to justify the whole thing, and turned a lot of people who had been sympathetic towards them, against them. The ordinary guy, I'm sure, had a lot of respect for the Germans, for the way in which they'd pulled themselves up from the depths of depression of the '20's and '30's, and had turned themselves into this magnificent fighting nation. The murderous nature of the Nazi regime was not revealed. Let's face it – who cared about the Jews?

Bomb Aimer They had nothing to connect to and they walked like bloody sheep. I don't think any nation in the world would have done it like they did it. They kidded themselves on, from when they went into these railway carriages. They knew bloody fine where they were going. They say they didn't, but they knew bloody fine.

Where were they in Germany? They were nothing. They had used money as their country, and money was nothing

German Jew Germany was my home. It will always remain so, but so is England. I feel lovely when I go back to Germany. I've been back two or three times since, and I think it's absolutely lovely because it's childhood to me. And the Germans. And the language. You don't think I speak English as well as I speak German? The English language, at best, fits me like a glove, but the German language is like my skin.

Going back to Germany now and talking to Germans, it's like coming back to a strange tribe, funnily enough. A curious mixture of strangeness and homeliness. In one respect they're like my old schoolfriends. There's a Professor in Mainz (the university was reopened after the Second World War, Napoleon closed it down) who is very much like one of my schoolfriends in Germany who stuck to me loyally; was a member of the Centre Party – the catholic party – who graduated with me from that school and became a lawyer; was called up; fought on the Russian front. He had to join the Nazi Party even to become a lawyer but I can assure you he never lost his political sentiments. After the war he became what you might call a secretary of the Civil Service. They call them Ministerial Dirigent. This was in Rhine Westphalia, in Mainz. When my wife and I went to Mainz in 1955 he was there. He was subsequently promoted to a larger one up in Cologne. I've lost track of him.

It was lovely to come back in 1955. He got together all those school-friends still left, still living there, who'd been in the last few years in school with me. Some of them asked me how I could bear to live abroad. They couldn't understand how I could be a foreigner in a foreign land. Don't I owe loyalties? one of them asked me. I asked him whether I could be expected to owe loyalties to gas chambers, which of course produced terrific confusion and embarrassment. I said I didn't wish to embarrass my host, but if I was asked a silly question, it deserves a silly answer. But it was all very amicable, nevertheless. It seemed as if nothing seemed to have happened. Nothing at all. I must say that my own last form retained its complement of five or six chaps who remained loyal and didn't become Nazis until the end, until they graduated.

When the Jews were being persecuted in Germany Gentile friends would say to us "Yes, but you're not like the other Jews," and that has perpetuated itself even after the war. I lost . . . They came for my aunt. They rounded up all the Jews in Westphalia, where she was living. She committed suicide. She took tablets. Another aunt also took tablets. I lost two. I lost none in the concentration camps because fortunately my relatives were either already dead or had gone abroad.

There was not a Jew left in Mainz after the war. They were all rounded up. Nobody was left. They all went to Lublin and from there to Auschwitz. Now how do you keep a sense of humour about that? I don't know.

If you keep a sense of humour you are a moral coward. If you don't, you're an hysteric

English Jew Being a marine electrician I had my own little workshop. We had German prisoners of war in the camp. They used to come into my workshop. I used to put the kettle on and we had an electric fire which I made myself. We'd have a good old brew-up and a talk. We used to have political discussions all bleeding day. I had a lot of Trotskyist German literature such as *Germany, What Next?*, which I used to give to them. They used to read it and we'd discuss it.

This bloke comes in – "Bloody hell. Fancy discussing with

them, after all they've bloody well done." By that time one of the Germans could speak a bit of English. I said "If you want to discuss it, why don't you discuss it with them." "Got nothing to discuss with them, after all they were responsible for."

The German said "I want to ask you a question. Suppose you lived in Germany, if you didn't join the National Socialists you were suspect immediately. If your wife and kids were in jeopardy, would you have joined?" "No. No, I wouldn't." "So you'd have sooner gone to a concentration camp, would you?" "Surely if there were enough of you, he wouldn't have been able to do it." "Not enough of us could do it. We weren't armed. They were. You say we are responsible for Hitler, but you live in a so-called democracy and you elected a group of politicians who helped Hitler to come into power. Therefore, you're just as responsible as we are." "Don't you give us that." "Did you know what they were doing? Did you know they were sending arms to Germany? Do you know about the Siemens industry? Things like that?" By the time he was finished he didn't know whether he was coming or going.

Ex-POW Before I went into those camps I was completely naive, and I was bloody scared, but I still didn't believe that there were such things as concentration camps. After I had been in these camps, which were not concentration camps of course, I saw slowly, here and there, and realised that there was one hell of a lot of evil in Germany. I was very lucky to be where I was. When I realised that the stories of the concentration camps were true and not just British propaganda, I thought: God Almighty. What shook me was that I couldn't believe that any unit of people, en masse, could be so infernally bloody evil, like the Japanese.

On the other hand I got on well with the Germans. I swotted German and I got to know them and I realised that the average German soldier and the average civilian were just as bloody helpless, or as humane as we are.

To give an example. Some friends of mine were round the other night with a very true blue couple. These people are very anti-German still – you know "The Battle of Britain, and our gallant boys" – which I don't deny. Don't get me wrong. They say "It's no good you saying half of them didn't know."

Alright. There's a point in that. But this other person said "Wait a minute, before you go any further – you know all these immigrants in Britain – Pakistanis." "Oh God, yes." "Well what do you think about it?" What they thought about it is much the same as what I think about it, without being personal to the individual. It's not colour at all, it's pressure of population, but we won't go into that.

This chap and this girl said "Now what precisely have you or are you doing about it?" And they sort of looked. "Yes" he said, "In other words you're like everybody else – like me – in this country. We loathe it but we do nothing about it. It seems to us that we can't."

Well, there is your perfect answer about 'why didn't the Germans stop Hitler?' It isn't so easy as that, is it? What are you going to do to stop immigration here? What have you done, if you don't agree with it? Nothing. Nor have I. What are you going to do tomorrow? You think and think and think, but you can't do much about it, can you?

It takes a bit of guts and organisation for thousands of people to march up and say "Look – stop, Mr Hitler"

Or to tell the government to stop immigration. I'm talking about the average mass of people. Not extremists. You don't do anything, do you? There's your answer you see. What could the Germans do?

Chief Petty Officer I know most of us were very bitter after the war because we saw so many atrocities, but the thing is, we politely forget the atrocities that we ourselves carried out. This is why we got our arse kicked out of India. It so happens that I've been to all these places and it also happens that I've seen some of the atrocities we ourselves did on the Indians. To us they were just bloody slaves. Literally. We treated them like slaves. We kicked their arse if they dared to ask for a cigarette.

Another point I want to put to you is this: In the British Navy, as in all forces – army, airforce, etcetera – particularly in times of war, and particularly in times of action, the law – the KRR's[1] – was that if you refused to obey a superior officer's direct command after being warned three times in front of any witness, and you continued to refuse to perform this order, he was at liberty to shoot you dead on the spot.

What I want to put to you is this – "These bastard Germans" as people say, were exactly in the same predicament – rank and file – as we were. Whilst I know that atrocities were perpetrated these were from the ranks of people like Himmler and Hitler and the high-ranking officers, and it was handed down. The German forces were much more strict on discipline – you weren't allowed to think for yourself at all. All you had to do was obey and die. So therefore I don't like people saying "Bastard Germans" or anything like that, because they were in exactly the same position as we were. They were fighting for their country. They were misled. But Christ, so were we.

---

[1] King's Rules and Regulations.

---

24 The only thing I'm annoyed with Hitler for was he took seven years of my life when I ought to have been doing all the daft things that people are doing now

London Woman The only thing I'm annoyed with Hitler for was he took seven years of my life at a time when I ought to have been doing all the daft things that people are doing now. We lost our youth.

London Man I've often said to the boy "You're lucky. When I was your age I had to go in the forces." I had to go. From 19 to 24. Them years was taken away from me. I couldn't please myself what I done. If I went and had a tooth out without telling anybody I was put on a charge – all that silly nonsense.

Glasgow Man When they were changing the paybooks I was the only person who had *Duration of War* on my paybook. I had to step forward, and when I stepped forward the whole company was standing behind me. I was the only one with

are standing behind me and everyone's going "You bloody
mug you!" That was the kind of thing that showed me nobody
wanted to volunteer. It's as blunt as that. My whole argument
is the nation had no time for the volunteer. I'm no saying they
didnae now and again use him when they wanted to save their
face. They'd use him. "We done this." Pick the guy out who
was a volunteer. Why did the saying "You, you and you" come
up? Because Britain's the greatest propaganda merchants in
the world. I still think they are. They attack themselves and
laugh at themselves. But it's done in a way as a cover up, to
cover our faults. The reason they went "You, you and you"
was because they knew there were no volunteers around.

If this country was a nation of sacrificers it was because they
were forced to do something that they obviously didnae want
do, and they done it with a great deal of reluctance and I would
say, without going any further, that's the myth chopped.

The answer could be, and I've heard it said, that people
could have kicked against it, despite the fact they were forced.
That it was open for them to object. But they didn't do it. They
were too old in the head! It just doesnae work. People are
afraid.

When a guy says to you "Mr Morrison, we've got a war here,
and you're a person we want to fight for us. Will you please
come and fight for us? If you don't come, you'll get a fine or
you'll be put in prison. You'll maybe get ten years. We might
even shoot you." I think it's easier without the emergency
powers, like they had during the war, to protest, but in this
country, despite all the talk, we don't protest easy. We allow a
£10 fine to deter us. But with a ten years prison sentence or a
prison sentence that's indefinite, like some of the COs got – a
year in prison, ready to come out, give them another year, that
kind of thing and pile it on – I would suggest that's more of a
deterrent than the fear of possibly dying. It was the threat that
they knew, rather than the one they didn't. For instance, I
don't think a lot of guys would ever have jumped out of an
aeroplane if they hadnae been sure in their mind that their
parachute would open – yet they didnae even know if you know
what I'm getting at. It's more fear, than anything else. If

Churchill instead of his blood, sweat and tears thing had said "Any man or woman in the forces who would like to give it all up and go home, can" – he wouldnae have got the microphone out his mouth before he'd been trampled to death in the rush.

2nd London Man I resented that some bloody stupid politicians bring wars about knowing bloody well they're too old to go themselves. I thought that it was an imposition that I should be yanked out of civvy street and put into something I didn't want to be part of, but I also had the sense to realise that I couldn't beat the army. So if you can't beat them, join them. And I made the best of it. But nothing on earth would make me like it. Nothing.

Liverpool Woman When I look back at that period they were happy times. I can honestly say I enjoyed them years better than I do now. Everyone was more friendly with each other. The way it is now, everyone says "Oh, bugger you" and draws the curtains. I'm the same. I don't talk to a soul in the street. It's not right to live like that is it?

3rd London Man Being involved in a war must be the worst time in anybody's life. But how can you say? – If there hadn't been a war, there might have been a bigger depression. I could have been worse off, because you must admit, it was only the war that cured the depression.

2nd London Man Life has been better since the war. Say, you've got a television – you expect it. My wife and I have worked our guts out to get a little car. In the old days, if somebody had a car, he's got to be well heeled. There's been a social revolution. The so-called better class can't get away with it – with walking all over you. It may not have been a completely good thing inasmuch as the bloody ignorant people like to rule the roost, and I'd hate to see the country run by this socialist mentality. I wouldn't vote Labour if it was the only party. At the same time though, the people I meet up the West End, (when I'm delivering their laundry) – Lady this and that – if they had their way mate, they'd have you back to your bloody cap and apron. "Stand to attention when I'm talking to you!" They don't like the evening up of the other class.

Leeds Man Once the war in Europe was over I was only too eager to get out of the army. As I couldn't, I took the opportunity of doing a bit of studying and managed to get to Welbeck College and to Cambridge University for a couple of months. This was an officers' course and I was the only non-commissioned officer there.

One day I listened to one old geezer, a Professor Benjamin who was lecturing about the Atlantic Freedom – the four freedoms. When he's finished I said "You've left out all the important freedoms." "What freedoms do you mean?" "Have you ever clocked on?" "Pray elucidate sir." It sounded as if it came out of a book. "Clocked on – punched a card." "What do you mean – punched a card?" "Let me tell you. In order to earn your living, to eat, and to pay your rent, you've got to take a card and drop it in a slot and press a lever that puts a time on it, in the morning. And before you leave for lunch, you've got to do it again. And if you don't do it you'll lose wages. And when you come back from lunch you have to do the same again. And if you don't you lose half an hour's wages. And at night time if you don't do it, you may lose half a day's wages. You've got to punch that card four times a day, five and a half days a week, all the year round. That's what I call economic freedom – you're a slave to the clock, and yet you never mentioned the clock." The poor old man didn't know anything about economic freedom – he'd always enjoyed it. "Oh" he said "We'll deal with that later on." That was round about 1945. We're still dealing with it.

Fords Shop Steward It's common knowledge isn't it that at the end of the war we came out the worst end of it. From about five years after the war Germany was way ahead of us. Economically. In this country we're dependent all the time on people in the Houses of Parliament. You've either got a Labour Government or you've got a Tory Government. They're both as bad as each other. What we want now is a complete change of the system, based on the welfare of the workers of the country. Not as it is at the moment. I think this country needs not necessarily Hitler, but it needs a man like him.

Liverpool Woman I don't think there was much unemployment after the war. I don't remember my brothers being out of a job. If you notice the way it is now, regards unemployment – it happened in the 1930's, building up to the war, and the war created work. There was plenty of work for everyone. You

"They called you up, and away you went. Basically, people don't want to bloody fight."

wonder, is it going to build up to the same thing now? Because something's got to break somewhere.

Teesside Man People don't want to fight in this country now. During the war, a man that didn't want to fight, he didn't know the answer. He didn't know the way out. They called you up, and away you went. Basically, people don't want to bloody fight. The biggest blow made for that was Cassius Clay, when they took his world champion. He was world champion boxer and they conscripted him for Vietnam and he said "No. I have no quarrel with those people. Those are my brothers." He got that publicity then. Nobody could question his integrity. He wasn't a coward. You've got that attitude now. I've got a son – 21 – and he'd never fight. They'd never conscript him.

Manchester Man The bloody slaughter and torture that went on, and is still going on in all parts of the world – it's got to stop. They thought the 1914–18 war was the war to end all wars, like the last was. They didn't know it's all got to go on forever more until people turn round and say "Here you are, here's a bloody sword each – go and fight out in that field, and whoever wins, let us know. That will do us." I honestly believe people will get together. I think this has to come.

4th London Man Looking back on it I feel there's no hope at all, frankly, for civilisation. Politics really is the end of everything, to me, because you're such slaves. There's no hope for the future at all. It really does distress me. I would love to think that someone, somewhere learnt some sense out of the last war, and individually a lot of people have. But people seem powerless. Perhaps I'm too cynical. We haven't had an atom war yet.

2nd Liverpool Woman I don't think a lot of people could have lived through the war if they'd have known what it was going to be like. It seems as if it was all in vain, doesn't it?

25

Royal Engineer I lost mates. But a lot of it was not when we were going into attacks. The first six, half dozen was three weeks after D day. We dug into this field by the side of this river, by Bénouville Bridge. They was laying out there sunbathing, which they shouldn't have done really. I'd been on guard the night beforehand. I was off. I was laying in my hole. I'd dug a hole in the ditch and put a door over the top.

They was laying out there sunbathing and they slung about a dozen 88 shells – which was his favourite gun, that 88 gun. You could hear it for miles. You'd hear it go: "Pop-pop" and "Whizzz" and "Crack!" – Big loud "Crack!" I heard them all hollering and I jumped up and run out.

The driver of my section, he had his leg blown off, back of his head smashed in and he was hollering and shouting. I run over and covered him up with a blanket. You couldn't do nothing else. There was our Corporal, he never had no shirt on, he was sunbathing and he got up and run to save a little kid that came out a farmhouse. A lump of shrapnel hit him in the back, and came out his chest. He was laying there, sqealing. And there was a sergeant. He had a big old jackknife in his belt. A bit of shrapnel had hit that and pushed it into his back.

We loaded them on the three ton lorry. We went down the first aid post, which was a big hole dug in the ground with a canvas over it. They took them in there and they all died in there.

West Country Girl I remember the first woman who had her husband killed in the village. I thought about that a bit. The ——— Bank was opposite where I worked, and he was a bank clerk there. She used to come to work with him every morning. They used to stand in the doorway, hugging and kissing good-bye. She had two little children when he went. He was about the first one to get killed and I thought that was awful, because they had been so in love. You could see it.

Liverpool Mother One very, very bad night during the Blitz we hadn't gone to the shelter. We had stairs in the kitchen, and there was a cupboard affair under the stairs and in there I used to put a mattress down. I'd put our two little ones in the cot, with one of the old-fashioned tabletops, that you could lift off the table, over the top. We didn't have a bathroom, so I had our ——— sitting on the table, washing him down, and a bomb came down and all the windows came in on top of him. I consoled him and there was a hammering at the door. I took him with me, with a towel thrown over him, and it was the chap opposite with a boy over his shoulder. He'd been caught in the blast and brought him in. I didn't think anything. We had a parlour and a kitchen. He brought him into the parlour and when he put the boy on the settee – he's got no head. Our ——— seen that and he went into a fit. He was fairly shaken by that.

RAF Ground Gunner When the V2's were dropping I was still in the RAF regiment. We were pulled up at a place just the other side of Romford. A place called Stapleford Tawney. It was a little aerodrome. There was us and another squadron. We'd gone up there to get the guns all made up again, and to recoup. One night there was a camp dance and I went to it. I was dancing with this little Waaf out of the office, a little girl with glasses. We had the dance on the Sunday.

On Tuesday, four o'clock in the afternoon we had Bofor guns, and I was No. 2. We was in this hangar and the other squadron was in the other hangar. Four o'clock it was my turn to do No.4 – that was the bloke who loaded the shells in. I'd jumped up onto the gun and I was just reaching down for a clip of shells and all of a sudden it was bedlam.

I was flat on my back and I was looking up, and there was all the corrugated sheeting falling down off the hangar. There was blokes lying all over the place, and smoke everywhere. We all rushed out to the aerodrome. The other hangar was flat. The rocket had gone straight on it. The Squadron Leader, an old boy with glasses, he's standing there with his arm twisted back – back around the back of his neck and he's crying "Oh my boys, oh my boys."

We all rushed into this hangar. Well, I rushed in and I stopped, cos the bloke who was my opposite number to me was sitting on the seat, and all he had was from his chest down. His head and shoulders is gone and there was all steam coming out. And there was a bloke's legs sticking out from underneath of the gun. I got hold of the feet and I was pulling them, but that's all I was pulling – the feet. I started vomiting. I run out, and as I run out I saw a Waaf lying on the floor. Somebody was just putting a sheet over her and it was this Waaf I'd been dancing with. She was face down on the floor but her feet were pointing skywards.

They sent the Waafs on the switchboard home and me and a Corporal was put on the switchboard. There was a Sergeant in ————— Hospital, he was dying and his wife kept phoning up. Everytime she phoned, it was muggins who was taking the calls. I didn't know what to say. I kept saying to her "As far as I know your husband is in ————— Hospital, and we're waiting for reports."

This went on for about an hour then I went out for a cup of tea and this Corporal took over. He was as thick as a bloody wall. She came on, and we'd just heard that he's died. As she came on he said "Sergeant So and So? Oh yes, it's just come through. He's dead." Just like that. I thought: You bastard. I went back and said "What do you want to say that for?" I could have smashed him. They lost half the squadron. A lot of our blokes went into ————— Hospital with shock. It's a wonder I didn't go myself, the way I rushed into that hangar and stopped. I can still see it now. That bloke sitting there.

Afterword

I wanted, when I set out to do this book, to examine the various "myths" of the 2nd World War, to see how they stood up to people's recollections of those years. The motivation for doing this the knowledge that there was a sizeable gulf between the British war films that I had been fed on as a schoolboy (Kenneth More, Dirk Bogarde and Jack Hawkins equipped with Tootal cravats and stiff upper lips against the might of the Nazi war machine) and the often uncritical television documentaries and nostalgic 2nd World War books that are still produced, as opposed to the stories that I heard when I went out to work many years ago. For someone born in 1945 it came as a shock, for instance, to hear Churchill and Montgomery talked of in derogatory terms – but even what I heard didn't really prepare me for some of the revelations and attitudes that I encountered when doing this book.

The brief I gave myself was to examine as many of the myths as I could and to try and cover the whole of the British Isles. Forty-nine people were interviewed, and one could argue that this is a ludicrously low number for a book that attempts to redress the balance. Further, those who find aspects of it disturbing will perhaps understandably suspect that those that I interviewed were hand-picked, either because theirs was a minority experience or because they had a sensational tale to tell.

Frankly, I believe that I've merely prodded a massive iceberg, and that if I were to interview 490 people the same basic picture would emerge. Of the 49 that I interviewed only three had a story to tell that I already knew in brief outline – Churchill's approach to the Communist Party and the RAF mutiny on Gibraltar, for instance, were unknown to me when I went to interview the people concerned. The three stories that I did superficially know were the anarchist on trial for disaffection, the German refugee shipped out to Australia, and the child evacuee starved to malnutrition.

As hard as it may be for some people to believe, when doing

the chapter on male war workers, for instance, I did not search out someone with a particularly bolshie outlook – I was simply looking for a miner, a factory worker, a docker, and so on. Their occupation, rather than their outlook, was my sole criteria. Similarly, when doing a chapter on the RAF, I simply looked for someone who had been in bomber command, and so on. I was only selective on a couple of occasions – the West Indian volunteer was one of them, when doing the chapter on the overseas volunteer. The contribution of Anzac and Canadian forces is well known, but the contribution of West Indians – in popular war mythology – is virtually non-existent. The same goes for the part played by Indian troops in the North African campaign and the contribution to the British war effort by Irish volunteers.

Those who served in North Africa, or in the RAF, or the Royal Navy will know of the presence of the above, and I believe that the majority of people who endured the last war will find within this book experiences that mirror their own, but rarely see the light of day. Although I mentioned British war films rather derogatively, a small minority do in fact give an accurate picture of what life was like in, for instance, the British Army. *The Hill* is a good example, even if it tends to suggest that the brutal treatment meted out was the result of a couple of sadistic NCO's, rather than part and parcel of army life. Some war novels also tend to give a truer picture, and books like *The Songs and Ballads of World War II* by Martin Page (Hart Davis, MacGibbon) also redress the balance. Against the nostalgic rehashes it has to be pointed out that, of course, there has grown a substantial body of serious work that critically examines the British war experience – *Living Through The Blitz* by Tom Harrison (Collins) and Angus Calder's *The People's War* (Jonathan Cape) are two examples.

The majority of those interviewed for this book were friends of friends, a minority were either friends or ex-workmates of mine whose war experiences they'd never told me, such as the Royal Engineer who landed on the first wave of D day, and in one instance the result of a letter to the anarchist periodical *Freedom*. Of those interviewed seven had had, or continue to have an active affiliation to left-wing political groups. All interviews were taped, with their permission. Most interviews lasted about two to three hours, though some extended up to six hours. With one exception they all took place in their homes, usually without other members of the family present.

One definite advantage I had in dealing with oral recollection, as opposed to corresponding with people, was a greater frankness in what was said, and the ability on my part to cross-examine. It also helped that it soon became apparent to the majority that I interviewed that I had often shared a similar work background, and this led to further frankness and intimacy in recollection for instance, about fiddling and skiving, which otherwise might not have been forthcoming.

Once the interviews were completed I then went about editing the transcribed tapes into a narrative. Obviously a tremendous amount had to be edited out, but I chose not to tamper around with transcribed material that went in. Only for the sake of narrative flow and clarity did I transpose paragraphs.

The main criteria for what went in, besides its interest value, was that it had to be first-hand experience, rather than hearsay. The one exception in the book is the alleged beating to death of a Polish airman. I included that partly because it's possible that it happened, but also to indicate that someone could believe that it had happened, which brings me to the question of historical accuracy.

This book is about people's first-hand experiences. The fact that someone might get a detail wrong is not going to invalidate the experience, for instance, of what it was like to land on Bénouville beach, for that individual, nor is that individual's recollections and feelings necessarily peculiar to him or her. I didn't meet one person, for instance, who didn't have a strong distaste for the pettiness of army life. Further, the way an individual chooses to remember something, or offers an opinion i.e. that Rommel was an officer and a gentleman, in itself tells us something about the feelings and attitudes of people who often reluctantly made history – the history of dates and battles, the history of the strategies of the pcliticians and the generals. This book is really about their own history – the way they reacted to the strategies of those politicians and generals.

Two omissions in the book are Dunkirk and life in prisoner of war camps. Both are continual sources of inspiration – the former for politicians (appeals to the "Spirit of Dunkirk") – and the latter for film and tv scriptwriters. As is indicated in this book, RAF flying crew were escape orientated, for economic reasons as much as anything else, and it would seem, from one report that I have heard, that the German authorities cleverly exploited class differences in at least one POW camp by penalising the other ranks every time one of the officers attempted to escape.

Dunkirk is a more serious ommission, because there is a body of evidence to suggest that in many cases officers virtually ditched their troops in the rush to the coast. This is not to denigrate or belittle those who did stay at their posts, who one presumes were in the majority. But the reports of individual officers scuttling off persist, as in the case of a despatch rider who was ordered off his motorbicycle by an officer who promptly got on it and drove off in the direction of the coast, leaving him stranded. Another interesting story, which I haven't substantiated, is that returning troops had any loss of kit docked off their pay. If true it would certainly go some way to explaining why appeals to the "spirit of Dunkirk" usually fall on deaf ears.

Whilst on the Dunkirk spirit it's worth mentioning an interesting article by William Rankin that appeared in *New Society* (15.11.73) "What Dunkirk Spirit?" He quotes a Ministry of Information report of the period which stated that morale was one of gloomy apprehension and that working-class women were said to be complacent about Hitler. One was overheard to say "He won't hurt us. It's the bosses he's after." Compare this with the commercial traveller on the Tube to Edgware who heard people arguing that Britain should cave in to Hitler as they had nothing to fear, it was the Jews he was after.

I'm aware just how much more work needs to be done, work that is outside the scope of this book. For instance, it would be a useful exercise to look at levels of absenteeism during and after the blitzes. My guess is that absenteeism increased after the blitzes, despite the fact that the Essential Works Order was amended in 1942 so that persistent cases of absenteeism became an offence. High factory attendance is sometimes given as an indication of the determination of the British people to get stuck into the job of defeating Hitler, and that such levels of attendance were particularly high, considering the disruption, after air-raids. But as one Liverpool women put it to me – what was the point of being absent from work when one's house had no windows, and possibly no gas, electricity or water. On the other hand the factory offered a shared communal experience and quite often warmth, tea and food. It should also be remembered that in some industries workers were earning phenomenal amounts of money. One semi-skilled teenager was earning more in 1944 than I was earning in 1964. Who wants to dodge work when there's good money to be made!

Another unanswered question is just how serious was the reluctance of the conscripted forces to fight. The book amply displays the big stick that was always ready for those who might have second thoughts – Lack of Moral Fibre; 84 days for paratroopers who refused to jump, and so on, but more interesting would be a study of mutinies in the services.

The RAF mutinies in the Near East around 1945–46 caused by disgruntlement about demobilisation have come to light fairly recently, but one can be sure that this is only the tip of a general pattern that existed throughout the war. The RAF mutiny on Gibraltar, the mutiny on the returning troop-ship and the mutterings of a transport section in North Africa would seem to indicate this. Although these mutinies were triggered off by a sense of injustice – as was the refusal of 191 men of the 51st Highland Division to obey an order at Salerno in 1943, leading to three sergeants being sentenced to death[1] – I would suggest the underlying cause was a general resentment at being conscripted in the first place. Although not mentioned in the book, the anarchist I talked to pointed out that the civilian prisons he was in were chock-a-block full of deserters. In 1947 there were still, according to the authorities, 20,000 wartime deserters at large. The figure, if anything, was probably higher.

There are indications that many exploited the confusion of Dunkirk and the 1944/45 Allied advance into Germany to officially "disappear". Even when this was not the case, the authorities sometimes inadvertently helped them. One soldier, rescued from the beaches of Dunkirk, returned to his Liverpool home on leave to find that his relations had been told that he was missing, presumed dead. Had it not been that an illegal gambling club was raided by the police four years later, no-one would ever have been the wiser.

I would suggest that the British war effort was maintained on the basis of threat and coercion, rather than on any volunteer spirit that prevailed amongst the majority of the population.

---

[1] The other 188 men received terms of hard labour, anything up to 10 years. Although the death sentences were eventually commuted, all these men served prison sentences. Their plight was highlighted in *The Secre Mutiny*, a documentary broadcast in December 1980 on BBC Radio 4, based on material collected by George Hume and produced by Geoffrey Cameron and Daniel Meikle of BBC Radio Scotland. Press reports first appeared in *Reynolds News* in 1959 and the *Sunday Mail* in December 1979.